"Did You Miss Me?"

Skip just gave me the look. "Guess."

I still got a tingle when Skip talked like that. I saw him almost every day at practice, at lunch, and at my locker, like now; but I guess I'd never get used to the idea that I was his girl. "I had a good time in New York," I said.

"Yeh? Meet any guys?"

"Skip!" I gave him a playful punch. "We went sightseeing and to plays. . . ."

I turned to see who or what it was that caught Skip's attention down the hall. Liz. Liz Halston. She passed out of our view.

"You were saying?" Skip asked, his eyes resting on me again.

"Oh, nothing."

He brushed my cheek with the back of his fingers. I think he might have kissed me, but just then a custodian rounded the corner and that sort of killed the romantic mood.

Books by Stella Pevsner

AND YOU GIVE ME A PAIN, ELAINE
CUTE IS A FOUR-LETTER WORD
LINDSAY, LINDSAY, FLY AWAY HOME
SISTER OF THE QUINTS

Available from ARCHWAY Paperbacks

ME, MY GOAT, AND MY SISTER'S WEDDING

Available from MINSTREL Books

CUTE IS A FOUR-LETTER WORD

Stella Pevsner

AN ARCHWAY PAPERBACK
Published by POCKET BOOKS • NEW YORK

An Archway Paperback published by
POCKET BOOKS, a division of Simon & Schuster Inc.
1230 Avenue of the Americas, New York, NY 10020

Published by arrangement with Houghton Mifflin/Clarion Books
Library of Congress Catalog Card Number: 79-23626

ISBN: 0-671-68845-6

First Archway Paperback printing September 1981

17   16   15   14   13   12   11   10

AN ARCHWAY PAPERBACK and colophon are
registered trademarks of Simon & Schuster Inc.

Printed in the U.S.A.

IL 7+

For Jim Giblin
and Marjorie Naughton

CUTE
IS A
FOUR-
LETTER
WORD

ONE

THIS WAS GOING TO BE THE YEAR OF THE CLARA.
I know the words don't have much by way of a musical ring, but what can I say? My name is Clara and this was going to be my year.

I came to that great decision one day last August, about a week before school was due to begin. Of course, to grown-ups who break out a new calendar, along with bottles of this and that, the new year begins ... well, you know when.

It's not International Law or anything when the new year has to occur. Various nationalities and religions set up their own dates for new beginnings, and I'm thinking right now especially of the Chinese, who have their own time and even their own names, like Year of the Horse, Year of the Monkey and so on.

To kids, for sure, the new year really begins in the fall when school starts. So that's why I decided the time was right to begin again. Clara Conrad was

going to shine forth as herself for a change, instead
of as the girl who.

I guess the *girl who* needs some clarification.

For starters, I'm the girl whose mother is a grade
school principal. So what's the big deal? I'll give an
example. You have a substitute teacher, a pushover,
who can't handle the class. Some funny stuff goes
on. And when the day of reckoning arrives, who
gets the zero-in look with the I-expected-more-of-
you-people speech? Right. The daughter of the
principal of another school. Or say, just for argu-
ment, said daughter tries to ease things for the substitute. You know what happens. Glares, sneers,
Miss Goody-Goody remarks.

Granted, the substitute situation is a sometime
thing, but every day a principal's kid has to decide
whether to go along with the crowd, hang back, or
be neutral.

That's one thing. Another is that I'm the *girl who*
has an older sister with a fantastic talent. Laurel is
eighteen, and when she plays the piano you could
swear someone had slipped a Horowitz on the turn-
table. Not that I, personally, can snap out the name
of the exact performer. I'm just giving an example.

Laurel, who drifted through her school years in a
dreamlike state, became like a person possessed
when seated at the piano. Over and over, chords,
scales, sections of a work. When I was younger, it
used to make me want to bang my head against a
wall.

Angel (she's my best friend) asked me just last
year how I could stand it, and I asked, "What?"
because by then Laurel's playing had become a
house sound like a refrigerator humming or a furnace
kicking on. But having a someday-famous pianist

2

going at it all the time had a somewhat unnerving effect on kids who stopped by.

Actually, not many kids did stop by. Not only because of the aforementioned reasons, but also because I was the *girl who* had the unenviable job as practically full-time after-school baby-sitter to one Jay Frank Fogarty.

I inherited Jay Frank, the kid next door, when he graduated from nursery school into kindergarten and have been stuck with him ever since. His mother, Sheri, who is looked down on by some of the neighbors because of her candid way of expressing herself, works at a data processing place and gets home around six. She's divorced. So Clara Conrad, sitter-next-door, has been rushing home from school for the past four years, cutting herself off from extra-curriculars, losing out on fun times with the crowd, and missing out on the boy-girl events, rare though they were, that took place after school hours.

But this year, The Year of the Clara, was going to be different.

First, regarding Laurel, the constant sound-of-music syndrome was over because my sister had gone off to New York City where she was enrolled in the Juilliard School of Music. That place, in case you don't know, is the golden-oldie of the classical music scene. It's an *event* to be accepted at Juilliard.

Second, the idea of my being a principal's daughter had finally lost ground as a hot news item.

As for Jay Frank, he was like a Siamese twin who had finally, through the miracle of science, been cut loose from me. Actually, it was neither science nor miracle but rather a natural growth process. Sheri (she's always let me call her that) had decided that her son, now going into fourth grade, was finally capable of unlocking a door, getting his own after-school snack, and amusing himself until she got there. So that left me home free. Home, free to do as I liked. And I was going to make the most of it. Put myself first, for a change.

"Clara, Clara!" I actually said the words aloud, alone in the house that afternoon. "This is your year! You will make yourself so memorable that even the most jaded of teachers (and I could name a few) will sigh as you stride across the stage for your diploma and say, 'We shall never see the likes of her again, not in our lifetime.'"

"You will make your home such a hot-shot place for social carryings-on that people will fight for standing room on the Clara Conrad scene. And you will meet HIM. The one. The boy who will win your heart and the right to have his name printed in waterproof marker on your gym shoes." It was all going to happen!

Barefooted, I raced into the living room, leaped on and off the sofa, spun around, and with arms outstretched fluttered out to the hall. Then leaning forward, using hands as well as feet, I mounted the stairs. At the top, one arm raised, I made a proclamation: "Citizens, you have just seen the Year of the Frog, the Year of the Butterfly, the Year of the Monkey. You are now about to witness . . . the Year of the Clara!"

And that was the afternoon of the evening I first heard about Halcyon.

TWO

I WAS CROUCHED OVER THE NEWSPAPER ON THE living room floor, checking out the movie ads. Mom was sitting on the piano bench, idly leafing through some sheets of music. I hoped she wasn't thinking of picking up her playing where she'd left off years ago.

"Clara," she said sort of hesitantly, "there's something I want to talk to you about."

I put my finger on the point I'd reached in the listings but didn't look around. The thought came to me, Oh, boy, she's going to ask me to take lessons again, disregarding the fact that even Laurel agreed years ago that I was a lost cause as far as music was concerned.

"Mom," I said, "I can read music, I know what it's about, but I can't play it, I don't want to play it." I ran my finger down to the next listing.

"Oh, stop. This has nothing to do with piano lessons. I want to talk to you about a letter that came today."

5

I turned around. "Is something wrong with Laurel?"

"Nothing at all. But there may be some changes in her plans, and you and I are directly involved. If you'll just put that paper away and give me your attention, I'd appreciate it."

There were only a couple of more movies, and even at a glance I could see the big R ratings, like most of them these days. I flicked the paper aside and flopped into a chair. "What's up?"

Mom seemed about to say something about my flip attitude (I know that look in her eye), but she let it go.

"Annie Schuyler wrote. You remember her, don't you? My old sorority sister from back East?"

"Sure. She brought me my little jeweled cat statue that time. Is she still in the decorating business?"

"She is, but that's not what she's writing about. She has an only niece, of whom she's very fond, and that niece has a daughter. A daughter your age."

I couldn't see what all this had to do with us or with Laurel, but it was clear that Mom was building up to something. I sat there waiting.

"Annie's niece and her husband have an art gallery, and for a while it did very well, but now with the economic crunch it's on relatively shaky ground. They're having to cut back on their life style, and one of the things they feel they can no longer afford is to send their daughter to an expensive boarding school."

I can't explain how at that moment I knew it, but I did. This boarding school girl was the threat, the thing the letter was all about. Still, I sat there waiting. Waiting to hear what was coming next.

Mom, for once, looked a little bit at a loss, as she

picked up a blue envelope lying just above the piano keys. Mom usually is in pretty good command. She has to be, dealing with kids and teachers and parents the way she does. She's old, in her late forties, and looks old, with that braided-bun hair-do and her stout figure. But nothing seems to shock her or rattle her, and I guess she's tops when it comes to dealing with tricky situations. So now, seeing her look of indecision, I got kind of nervous.

"Mom," I said, "what is it? What's the letter about?"

She looked at me directly. "Clara, we've always lived comfortably, thank goodness, and I've never had to touch the insurance your father set aside for the education of you girls. But he couldn't have known at the time he died how expenses would rise through the years."

"Do we . . . do we have to sell the house?" I knew a girl whose folks had done that. The thought was terrifying. Our house was a white elephant in a way, and maybe too big for the two of us, but it was the only home I'd ever known.

"Oh, the house." Mom gave a little fan of the letter. "We're better off hanging onto this, with the tax situation as it is. No, it's Laurel. Her expenses. The bills are just horrendous. Oh, Clara, don't get alarmed," she said, as I leaned forward. "We'll manage, somehow we'll manage. It's just that now something has happened that can at least lighten the load of her expenses."

If that was the case, why this heavy conversation? Again, some signal came through to me. There was a catch. There was a catch that somehow involved me. And that girl. That girl my age. I just couldn't make the connection between her not being able to afford boarding school and our being able to afford sending my sister to Juilliard. "Can I read the letter?"

"May I," Mom said automatically. I swear, she'd correct my grammar if I were on my death-bed. "Yes, you may," she said, taking the pages from the envelope, "or I could just tell you. Annie tends to ramble."

"Then tell me. It can't be all that bad," I said, trying to lighten things up.

Mom's look shifted toward the window where, from beyond Jay Frank's house, there was open prairie. She looked back at me. "The girl I mentioned, the girl your age . . ."

Here it comes, I thought. The kicker. I tried to hold the smile.

". . . her name is Halcyon. She's attended boarding schools for years. She's accustomed to that type of school life. But, as I mentioned, her parents can't manage it this year. However, they've refused financial help from the aunt, my friend Annie."

So what was the big deal? "Don't they have schools she could go to in New York City? Isn't that where they live?"

"Yes, in an apartment near Lincoln Center. But Halcyon . . ."—Mom gave a slight twist of the lips—"Halcyon is making a tremendous fuss about going to a city school there for eighth grade. She says she'd be an outsider, and oh, I don't know what all, but whatever it is, her parents can't seem to handle it."

"Huh!"

"I know, it sounds peculiar, but I gather the girl has built up some kind of ego thing about boarding school that's kept her from making friends with the

8

two or three public school girls in her building, and she says she'd rather do anything than try to break in with them, as she puts it."

Tough toenails, I thought, but I didn't say anything.

"I guess you know what I'm getting at," Mom said.

"No, I don't." I honestly didn't right then. What did the problem of some snob kid in New York have to do with Mom and me?

"Well, here it is. Annie came up with a suggestion, and surprisingly enough, Halcyon agreed and so did her parents." Mom paused. "You see, if Halcyon came out to live with us she'd still be going to school out of state and could save face, strange as it seems. And, there wouldn't be the financial burden on her family."

I was so dazed by this development that I just let Mom's next words—". . . and Laurel could stay in the apartment with Halcyon's parents."—fly right over my head. Mom smiled. "It would be a kind of domestic student exchange program."

"Here?" I kind of croaked. "That girl wants to come live here? With us, in our house?"

"Well, it's big enough, goodness knows. And actually, the experience of attending a suburban school in the Midwest might be good for Halcyon."

"For her!" I leaped out of the chair. "And what about me? How's this supposed to affect my life?"

"Well, Clara . . ." Mom looked a bit disconcerted. "I should think it would be an interesting experience for you. Having a girl your own age . . ."

"A creepy kid who thinks she's too good for public school!"

"Now, just a minute. I didn't say anything . . ."

9

"You said she can't or won't or whatever make friends . . ."

"I know that may be hard to understand. But Clara, you've gone through all the grades with more or less the same classmates . . ."

"Don't think all of them like me!"

"Come now . . ."

"Well, I'm not exactly Miss Popularity. I mean, kids like me all right and I get along pretty well, but I've had things go wrong along the way. I didn't just ease into where I am now." I knew I was babbling and more or less contradicting myself. What I meant and couldn't come out and say was that I'd had to work and work hard to prove I was a regular kid even if my mom was a principal and half my life was tied to babysitting. "They ought to just *make* her go to school there and take her knocks," I said, switching back to the real issue. "That's what I'd do, if I were the parents." I flopped back onto the chair.

Mom half smiled as she riffled the pages of the letter. "Basically, you're right, Clara. But it's not fair for you and me, out here, to make judgments. All we need be concerned about is the question of whether or not to accept the offer. That's what it amounts to."

"Does it amount to a lot of money?"

Mom hesitated. "Enough. Not an overwhelming amount, but I would say enough to make a difference."

I felt really rotten, and cornered. Rotten because I hated to agree, and cornered because I knew it was the only decent thing to do.

I lowered my head. "When would she come out?"

"School starts . . ." Mom's sentence ended in a

10

sigh. The staff, if you can believe it, dreads opening more than students, who tend to like the first couple of days.

"Very soon." I supplied her answer. "So all this is kind of sudden, isn't it?"

"Apparently the battle in Halcyon's family has been going on all summer, and everyone's been upset," Mom said. "Just recently, Laurel went to Halcyon's house on a visit with Annie, and somehow, the idea surfaced. Everyone out there thinks it's perfect."

"How about Laurel?"

Mom shrugged and smiled. "Oh, you know your sister. Give her a good piano and she's content as a clam, just anywhere."

Lucky Laurel. In a way I envied her for being so dedicated to one goal. On the other hand, I wouldn't want to have everything so clearcut. I wanted to experience a lot of things. I'd really meant it when I'd flung out my arms and raced around saying, "Here I am, world. Are you ready for me?"

"What are your feelings, Clara?"

I came back with a clearing of throat. "It's okay with me, I guess, if you guys . . . you grown-ups . . . work it out." Maybe it wouldn't work out. "As I said, it seems awfully sudden, but . . ."

"I'll call Annie, I think. And get a few more facts. And then call Laurel."

"Are you going to call the parents, too?"

"No, I should think they would call me."

That's what I was thinking. "Do you have a picture of that girl?" I couldn't bring myself to say her name.

"Of Halcyon? No. Why?"

"Just curious." She was probably a real gross-ball.

I faked a yawn, stood up, stretched, and mumbled something about going up to listen to some rock.

Mom took hold of my hand as I started to pass by, and pressed it against her cheek. "Clara," she said as I paused, "I know we haven't spent a lot of time together lately. I—well, I was looking forward . . ." She didn't seem to know how to put it so I helped her out.

". . . to a quiet year?" (I really didn't mean that as a slam against Laurel and her playing.)

Mom laughed. "Let's say I was looking forward to our having quiet times this last year of yours in grade school. Before . . ."

I guess she meant before I got involved in the hyped-up activities of high school. Little did she know I wasn't waiting. I was going to begin NOW.

"Oh, well." I gave her a light kiss on the cheek and tore upstairs.

But in my room, I stood, wondering. Was it really going to begin . . . my Year of the Clara . . . when I fully intended to fly free? Or would this Halcyon blast in like rough weather and send me into a tailspin?

Well, I wouldn't let her. I was going to be in charge. I was, I was.

I walked to the mirror and looked at my reflection. "You are, Clara," I told it. It didn't look altogether convinced.

THREE

T HE NEXT DAY MY BEST FRIEND, ANGEL BAR-clay, came over and Fergy McNutt trailed behind, looking agreeable as usual. Fergy is a fairly tall, thin kid with stringy hair and glasses and not much going for him in the looks department. That doesn't seem to make any difference to Fergy, and neither does the fact that behind his back, or even to his face, kids call him Nuttsy.

"What brings the two of you over here together?" I asked, putting it bluntly. I'd known both of them for years, but usually they didn't travel as a pair.

"We have a little proposition to put to you," Angel said, glancing around the backyard. "Do you mind if I sun myself while we talk? There isn't too much time left to set my tan."

She dragged our aluminum and plastic chaise from under the tree, flipped the pad over to the cleaner underside and, checking the sky, got out of her jeans and scoop-necked top. Her tan, going in all directions from the green bikini she had on underneath, looked pretty well set to me. And her shape was pretty well established, too.

Angel lay on her stomach and watched as Fergy and I dragged up webbed chairs to the edge of the shade and sat like spectators at a varsity show.

"Well?" I said, feeling kind of silly without knowing why. "What's the proposition?"

"Tell her, Fergy," Angel said, propping herself up on her arms and pulling at her bangs. Angel's bangs are separated at the center and pulled out to little blond wings at the side. They're like a trademark.

"Rats," Fergy said. "We want to raise rats." He tilted his white canvas hat forward to shade his eyes. "Preferably in your cellar."

I sat there for I don't know how many seconds.

"Well?" Angel finally said. "Do you have any objections?"

"Did you say . . . rats in our cellar?" I looked at Fergy, who was stretched as far as he could while still staying attached to the chair seat. "Why our cellar? And why raise rats at all?"

"Your cellar because our house doesn't have any, and Angel's is all fixed up as a family room." Fergy paused to let that register. "As for the rats, they're going to be our experiment for the science fair in January. We can get them from a lab, guaranteed free of disease."

"Oh, that's wonderful," I said. "I wouldn't want any diseased rats running around the house."

"They won't be running anywhere," Angel said serenely. "We'll keep them in cages. Won't we, Fergy?"

"I can get the cages, too," Fergy said. "The only

problem is space, and that's how come we thought of your cellar, Clara. You don't use it for anything that I can recall."

Angel lowered her head to the chaise and let her arms dangle over the sides. She picked at a blade of grass. "Your mother surely wouldn't object. I mean, it *is* an educational project."

"You guys! *I'd* object! I don't want those creepy little things in my house. Not for a science project or anything else."

"People can get quite attached to rats," Fergy said in his mild, agreeable voice. "Even people who as a general rule don't care for mice."

"Not me. I'd never get attached. And besides, what if you two got sick or busy or something and couldn't get over to take care of them? Huh? How about that?"

"Clara," Angel said. She gazed at me with those Botticelli blue eyes. The very eyes that had knocked over hearts like a row of dominoes, beginning with kindergarten, and which last year had claimed the undying affection of Skip Svoboda, basketball hero of Harrison Junior High. "Do you honestly believe that either Fergy or I would shirk our duties for any reason whatsoever?"

I couldn't honestly believe they would. Fergy had never missed a deadline as editor of the school paper, had never had to ask for extra time when a paper was due, and had never received anything but rave reviews at parent-teacher conferences. As for Angel, her fly-away heavenly looks were deceptive. She was a down-to-earth meat and potatoes person when it came to the banquet of life.

I have to tell you something about Angel Barclay.

15

She is as close to a programmed person as I ever hope to meet. To show you how planned she is, I can reveal this fact: Her name was picked out before she was even born, and her looks met the specifications. "What if you'd been a boy?" I asked her once.

"What ifs are a waste of time," she answered.

Fergy hoisted himself up. "If you don't mind, Clara, I'd like to check out the cellar for dampness. It's a long time since I've been down there. Also, I'd better check the ventilation."

"Check the cobwebs, while you're at it," I called after him. "And the grime."

"You're being surprisingly negative about this," Angel said. She gave a little shriek as she brushed an ant from her wrist.

"I just don't understand your sudden interest in science," I said. "Fergy, yes. He's the type all right. But you?"

"I've been revising my Plan. And science, I discovered is an area I've overlooked." Angel flipped to her back and spoke into the sky. "I'm giving up Pom Pon Squad, Clara. One year is enough. It doesn't get you anything."

"It got you Skip Svoboda."

"I've put a question mark after Skip."

"A *what?* You *mean?*" Stunned, I stared at Angel.

"Don't get me wrong. Skip's fine, for what he is. But . . ."

"Are you actually trying to tell me you don't like Skip any more?" The very suggestion nearly wiped me out.

"I like him. But there's really no place for him in my Plan. It seems this whole past year was kind of a waste. A floating thing. I need to get back to solid ground and fasten some moorings. That's why Fergy's science thing with the rats attracts me."

From Skip Svoboda to rats. Only Angel could ever consider a switch like that. Here *I* was, thinking of how I wanted to fly free this year . . . hang-glide my way through eighth . . . and here *she* was, just the opposite. "Angel," I said, "I find you hard to believe. Tossing all the good things aside, just like that. Everything I've envied." Just in time I added, "Like Pom Pon."

Angel squinted one eye against the glare of the sun and fixed the other on me. "You want to make Pom Pon?"

Did I want to make Pom Pon? Does a rock band want to hit the charts? Does a model want to make the cover of *Vogue?* "I wouldn't mind," I said.

"Then how about making a deal? If you turn over the cellar to us and our experiment, I'll turn over my position on the Pom Pon Squad to you."

My heart fluttered like a pennant. Need I tell you that getting into Pom Pon is every junior high girl's idea of paradise? The costumes, the excitement, the glory!

While I wasn't quite ready to accept the fact that even Angel could cast aside someone like Skip, the Pom Pon nix was possible. Angel had been into a lot of things, like chess, figure skating, weaving, Berlitz Russian. But as soon as she got good at them, she'd go on to something else. She'd been captain of the squad last year, so in her mind that could have been it for Pom Pon.

"You really mean it?" I said, staring. "You'd really turn over your place on Pom Pon to me?"

Angel gave a shrug that said, *Sure, why not?*

"But I've never even tried out."

"Clara, how could you? All these years tied up with little Pesty next door. You're free now. Free to turn cartwheels."

"Yeh. But Angel, once the word gets out that there's a place vacant you know what'll happen. There'll be such a mad rush of bodies I won't stand a chance."

"Leave that to me. I'll get you on. We'll have a few coaching sessions. I'll teach you all the tryout tricks, and I'll get you that position before the rest of the girls wake up and smell the Ovaltine."

With anyone else that would have been so much hogwash. But Angel means what she says. She's so organized that when she goes into action things fall into place for her. No question about it.

She has a Life Plan, a Weekly Plan, and a Today's Plan. She has a notebook with spaces marked off for each division.

I operate on a far simpler plan: Get through to-day. With the sub-head, Do Not Procrastinate. I'm terrible the way I put things off. Maybe if I made lists like Angel, I'd go ahead and get things done. But I put off making lists.

Angel let me look at her Life Plan once. It had things in it like:

Age 14–18 *High School*

Besides required courses, each year take a subject in a different field to test aptitude and interest.

Each year, different type of after-school and summer job.

18

Class President—junior year.

Visit colleges between junior and senior year. Make selection.

Senior year. Accept favorite college.

Age 18–22   Attend college.

Age 22   Graduate with honors.

Age 22–23   Year abroad, filling in cultural gaps.

Age 23–27   Get well established in career. Develop meaningful hobbies in preparation for enriched middle years.

Age 27   Marry (?)

Age 29   Have child (????)

"Why did you put the question mark after marriage?" I asked her. "Don't you think there'll be any single guys around by then?"

"The way things are going, there may not be *marriage*," Angel said. "No, really, you never know, so I don't like to plan ahead too far."

That was the day, I think, that I couldn't decide whether to walk to town and buy a birthday card for my aunt or just hang around the house and write a letter.

Fergy came back, slapping his canvas hat against his leg to knock off the cobwebs. "Place looks perfect," he said. "Just needs a little cleaning up. Okay if we come over Saturday?"

"Hey . . . I didn't say! Besides . . . my mother."

Fergy patted my shoulder. "You'll handle that okay. You leaving, Angel?"

She checked her watch. "I'm ready."

As she started putting her clothes back on, I thought of something. "Saturday? Saturday isn't so good. That's the day I'm getting a new sister."

You could hear the snap on Angel's jeans clink shut. "You're *what?*"

"On Saturday. I tried to call and tell you but you're always off somewhere."

Angel glanced toward the house. "New sister? What do you mean?"

"A live-in sister is what I mean I'm getting. Some kid from New York City. It's kind of a trade. Laurel's going to live with *her* parents."

"Isn't this kind of sudden?" Angel asked. "How old is she, anyway?"

"Our age. And sure, it's sudden. I'm not too thrilled about it, but what can I do?"

"What's her name?" Angel went on.

"*Hal*cyon." I made it sound nasal.

"Mmmm. Interesting."

"It's dorky," I said.

"Actually, it's Greek." Fergy furrowed his brow. "There was a goddess Halcyone, I believe, who pitched herself into the drink because . . . uh . . . because. I don't remember exactly. But it was probably over some guy. Goddesses were always doing themselves in over unrequited love."

"I wouldn't," Angel said.

"You're not a goddess, Angel," Fergy said. "Try to keep that in mind."

Before they got any further along on the kidding-insult routine, I broke in, "Halcyon's a boarding-school kid. And like me, she may not be hot on the idea of rats in the cellar. It's going to be hard enough for her to get used to living out here in the boonies. So don't take the rat deal as a sure thing, you guys."

Angel looked at me. "Pom Pon" was all she said.

I pictured those crimson sweaters and the white pleated skirts. And I could feel the tingle rising from my sneakers and jetting straight to my scalp as the applause bounced from the bleachers. I couldn't let all that slip by.

"If you could just put it off until next week?" I walked them toward the front yard. "On account of Halcyon?"

"Okay. Next week," Fergy said.

Angel gave a twist to her wings. "On account of Halcyon. I wonder, Clara, if you know what you're getting into with this girl."

I was wondering all right.

Angel and Fergy left and I returned to the back yard. I began thinking about how little control I had over my life. How could I have known a week ago that that kid from New York was going to come live with us? How could I have known this morning that we were going to have rat boarders in the basement? And could I have guessed, even an hour ago, that a terrific Pom Pon plum was about to fall into my frail little hands?

One thing was clear. The Year of the Clara was going to be one big bundle of surprises. So . . . I'd go with the flow and make the most of everything.

I started turning cartwheels, and you know what?

I was dynamite. "Watch out, world!" I said, reaching toward the sky.

It was a good thing I looked up at that moment. A bird was flying low and dropped a little excess baggage that just missed my head.

In every way, my life was dropping little surprises.

FOUR

AFTER THE CARTWHEELS, AND ESPECIALLY AFTER
the rat talk I felt like showering, but I'd promised
Mom faithfully that I'd clean out Laurel's room
today. ("Clara, just get at it.") After lugging those
boxes around I'd probably feel like another shower.

"Put everything away in categories," Mom had
ordered. "Clothes, books, and so on. Label the boxes
and then put them in the back of her closet."

"Why does it have to be today?" I asked in my
usual put-off fashion.

"Because."

Long ago, I'd learned there was no use arguing
when Mom used that particular tone.

I started with Laurel's closet. She had taken along
some summer clothes and most of her fall things. I
packed what was left into separate boxes, labeled
Summer, Fall, and *Winter.* We'd send the winter
things later.

My sister hadn't dreamed, when she left, that

someone else would be using her room, or I'll bet she'd have gotten rid of lots of stuff. But maybe not. There were no juicy notes or hate lists. Just programs from recitals, concert programs, music notebooks. I put it all into a box and labeled it *Nostalgia*. If anyone ever went through my stuff—and I cringed at the thought—they'd probably label it *Garbage*. But to each his own, I say.

I was about to tackle things from the tops of dresser, desk, and bedside table when I heard the Day Camp bus grind to a halt on the corner, followed by the yells of the escapees. As usual, a couple of minutes later, the front doorbell rang.

"Hey, come on in, Jay Frank," I yelled down the stairs. Since we don't have air conditioning, we do have direct contact with the outdoors, which can be fairly convenient at times.

I collapsed on the top step, and as soon as I heard the screen door slam, called out, "I'm up here."

Jay Frank came to the foot of the stairs, and I have to say that as grimy and sweaty as I looked and felt, I was Miss Plastic-Wrapped Perfection compared to Jay Frank. At best, he's kind of a sorry-looking excuse of a kid, with that skinny little nine-year-old body and a face that can only bring to mind the word "pathetic." Today, he looked like the last straggler from an obstacle course.

"Hey, Jay Frank, want to come upstairs and help?" He wouldn't be much help, but I had to keep on with the cleaning.

"Help with what?"

"Oh, well." I started down because habit is stronger than resolution, and I had long been in the habit of mother-henning Jay Frank.

"Rough day, huh?" I said, when I got the close-up shot of his thin face, awash with streaks of dirty sweat. The hair in front of his ears and along his neck was clinging in damp little clumps.

"I have a headache and the bus driver made the kids shut the windows when they started to spit out and then they sang *Ninety-Nine Cans of Beer on the Wall* real loud and they got down to seventeen before I got off."

If Jay Frank had told all that to his mother, Sheri would have said something like, "That's life, kid." It's not that she's insensitive. She just believes in toughening up her son's hide to ward off the slings and arrows of life, as they say.

"Come on out to the kitchen," I told him. "Hawaiian Punch fights headaches three ways."

We sat opposite each other at the kitchen table and split a can and discussed his day, which had contained everything guaranteed to de-energize kids so they'd pass out the minute they got home, because that's what the parents were paying for.

"I haven't had such a fun day, either," I told Jay Frank, after he'd recited his sorry tale.

"Whatcha been doing?"

I told him about all the work that had been piled onto me because of the Halcyon creature. Then I got around to telling him about the rats.

"I'll help," he offered, perking up. His face was a sight to behold, what with the dried sweat, the dirt, and now smears of pink around his lips. "I'll come over every day after school and . . ."

"Hey." I just had to interrupt him. "There's a new game plan, remember? I'm not going to be your sitter any more. That means . . ."

His face seemed to shrivel a little. "I know." He turned away on the chair, and I could hear the teentsy sound of shoe laces against the linoleum. Or did I just imagine it? At least one of his sneakers was always untied.

"I have to go home," he said to empty space. He picked up his glass and took it to the sink and washed it. That was another thing Sheri rammed home. *Pick up after yourself, kid.* He still had to lean forward slightly to reach the faucet and I thought, he's too little. It isn't right for him to be on his own. Not yet.

"Hang around a while," I said. "Keep me company while I finish Laurel's room. You don't have to help."

He touched the bump of his new house key under his T-shirt. "I guess I'll just go home and lie down a while."

"Hey, Jay Frank!" I said, faking excitement. "You did it after all my years of harping. Said *lie* instead of *lay!*"

"Chickens lay, people lie," he said, with a thin smile, repeating the phrase I'd told him over and over.

Not content with that progress, I pushed on. "And are you *lying* down or *laying* down?" Living with a principal leaves its mark.

"I'm not doing either," Jay Frank said with a steady look. "What I'm doing is leaving. Good-bye."

"See you," I said to the back of him as he let himself out. The screen door clicked shut, and I was left standing there.

I felt like a rat. A rat deserting a sinking ship. Jay Frank wasn't sinking, but all the same he didn't need that shove from me.

*   *   *

Because Mom is a firm believer in pleasant dinner conversation, I put my two pressing topics on hold until after we'd finished eating.

"Oh, by the way . . ." I started off as we were clearing the table. I stopped as Mom gave me a slightly alarmed look.

" 'Oh, by the way' is a phrase that makes parents wary," she said after a moment.

"Why is that?"

"Because it's often followed with words like, 'I'm to be a Stop Sign in the traffic play tomorrow and I need a costume.' "

"Mom! That happened way back in the third grade. Lately, I've felt more like *Yield* on the Highway of Life."

I thought I was doing pretty well saying that right off the top of my head, but Mom looked more taken aback than impressed.

"Would you care to explain that remark, Clara?"

Again, a snap answer. "Everyone always wants me to give way for their own convenience."

That hit the mark. *Halcyon*. I didn't have to say the word. Mom had no moss on her. "But it's not all that bad," I continued, "because I finally have a chance to do something *I* want to do." Meaningful pause. "I'm going out for Pom Pon this year."

"Pom Pon, Clara?" Mom looked truly surprised. "What suddenly brought that on? And is it something you want to do? Seriously, now?"

"Mom! Any girl in Harrison Junior High would shave her head bald to get on Pom Pon."

"I had no idea."

"That's because you're in K-6 where games are just games. Pom Pon's the real stuff, Mom."

"And the competition is keen, you say?"

27

"Deadly. But Angel's promised to help me. She's going to coach me to take *her* place." I stuck the plates into the dishwasher. "There's just one little thing . . . a kind of favor . . ."

"Yes?"

I almost hyperventilated with a single breath. "Angel and Fergy, in return, would like to set up a bunch of rat cages. With rats. In our . . . cellar?"

Mom stared. And stared. And stared.

"Don't you . . . don't you get it?" I was becoming a little disconcerted. "They use rats for experiments—scientists—and this is a school science fair project and . . ."

"Are you saying . . ." Now Mom's face was kind of puffed with unbelievability. "Saying that your friends plan to dissect animals here . . . in our house?"

"Dissect! Mom, what do you think they are, a couple of zombies on the loose? They just want to keep rats."

"For what purpose, precisely?"

I hadn't thought to ask, precisely, and that was really too bad. "Like I told you, for a science fair project," I said, as though she was at fault for not paying attention. "One of those little things they do . . . you know . . . for science fairs," I repeated lamely.

"Why our cellar?" I wasn't crazy about the tone Mom's voice had taken.

"Because they don't have any other place."

"Clara, did you tell them they could use our cellar, without even . . ."

"I said I'd have to talk it over with you, but I didn't see how you could mind, because it's educational."

28

"It's also smelly and a nuisance. And a responsibility."

"You know Angel and Fergy," I protested. "They're as responsible as anyone can get."

"Experiments. I don't like the sound of that word at all," Mom said.

I could see her point. And I could also see that crimson Pom Pon sweater and pleated skirt on someone like Doris Sycow, instead of me. "Behavior!" The word just leaped into my mind. "Animal behavior. That's what they're studying, or will, if you'll just . . ."

"Oh?"

"And you've got to admit that's very important for man . . . I mean . . . humankind. Why people—psychologists—learn all kinds of things from studying the habits of animals. Even if they are only rats."

"I see. When did this whole subject come up?"

"Just today. I told Angel and Fergy I couldn't make any promises until I'd checked it out with you." I sounded so self-righteous I couldn't believe it. What *had* I said, as a matter of fact? "But I told them you probably wouldn't mind." I remembered that much. "I also said they shouldn't count on anything until next week, after Halcyon gets here." I sniffed, just a little, to show how well I was bearing up under this handicap.

Mom poured dishwasher stuff into the compartment and set the dial. "Speaking of Halcyon, is her room ready?"

"Ummm." I'd never quite got back to it after Jay Frank left. "Partly. It's partly ready. I'll be sure to have it done before she gets here Saturday."

"Clara. Go up and finish it. Now."

I sighed. "All right. But could I call Angel first?"

29

"If it's vital."

"I've got to let her know, Mom. About the rats . . . the behavior experiment with the rats. Is it okay, Mom?"

Silence.

I looked around from the phone. Mom was standing like a giant post, eyes closed, a resigned look on her face. She was making a *Yield* sign with her fingers.

FIVE

MOM AND I STOOD BY THE WINDOW IN THE AIR-
port waiting area where Halcyon was supposed to
disembark, watching planes taxi in and out.

"How are we supposed to recognize her?" I asked.
"Did her folks send a mug shot?" If so, I hadn't
seen it. I was feeling pretty nervous about meeting
this kid face to face.

"No," Mom said. "But I doubt there would be
two girls your age traveling on this precise plane
alone. And she'll be on the lookout for us. I think
that's her plane now."

It seemed like forever as we watched the jet ma-
neuver into position. Finally people started trickling
down the carpeted corridor and into our area. Suddenly Mom said, "There she is!"

And there she was. There could be no doubt of it.

The girl I saw was about my height, but heavier.
She had long, dark hair smoothed back by a head-
band and wore tight pants and a fluttery Madras top.
All this was topped by a peevish look.

31

Her name (we'd looked it up) was Greek all right, and it meant calm and tranquil. Halcyon looked ready to explode. From her expression you'd think she'd expected a path to be cleared for her. Instead she was stuck in the mob, loaded down as she was with an overnight bag, purse, camera, and tennis racquet.

Mom started forward, like a tugboat through the crowd, and I bobbed along in her wake. Mom reached Halcyon, held out a hand in welcome, and after a bit of shifting, a hand reached out.

"And this is my daughter, Clara," Mom said as I shuffled up.

"Hi." I held out my hand and got the strap of a canvas bag hooked onto it. I almost pitched forward from the weight. "Is this everything?" I asked, really believing it was possible.

Halcyon gave me a withering look. "My baggage is *checked*," she said. "I just hope they didn't lose anything."

"We'll get it," Mom said, unperturbed. "How was the flight, Halcyon?"

"Terrible. You can just bet I'm going to have my father complain to the airline about the hassle they gave me about my things. Oh! My prints!" She dropped everything but her purse and camera and dashed over to a stewardess just emerging from the tunnel. The stewardess, looking none too pleased, went back toward the plane, with Halcyon following.

I lowered the bag to the floor and looked at Mom. "Calm. Tranquil," I murmured.

Halcyon came back carrying a cardboard carton with a handle attached. The stewardess walked over to the desk, said something to the man there, and they gave us the kind of looks that let us know we

32

were not all-time favorites. Halcyon started picking up her stuff.

"I'll carry the tennis racquet," Mom said, which was a smart move.

"I'll take something else for balance," I said, and reached out for the camera case.

Halcyon jerked back. "Oh, no. No one carries this but me. It's a Leica, and my father would go into cardiac arrest if anything happened to it. You can take this." She handed me a tote bag that practically pulled my arm out of the socket.

When we reached the luggage claim, Halcyon dragged out three bags, one of them super-size.

Blinking, Mom said, "I'll try to find someone to help."

She came back with a guy in uniform. "I'll get the car," she said. "You girls wait out at the curb with all this."

We waited a long time, Halcyon and I, in the heat of that Saturday noon, with the roar of the jets and the fumes soaking into every pore.

"I just can't believe this scene," Halcyon said, pacing like an executive. "Here I am, nauseated, and now this delay."

"I guess if they'd known, they'd have built the garage closer."

"In New York you don't have this kind of inconvenience. I need a coke. Where's the refreshment stand?"

" 'Way back inside. There isn't time."

Halcyon hoisted the biggest bag on end, sat on it, crossed her arms, and tapped her foot. I had the feeling that I could fade into the exhaust fumes and disintegrate and Halcyon would neither notice nor be able to give a description of me to the police.

"I'll have that tote bag over there," she said suddenly. "It's got my hair things in it."

I'll have. I really liked that. And yet I took the bag over to her.

Halcyon handed me a dryer, a curler, and then the bag, itself, after she'd pulled out a brush. She flicked off the tortoise headband and began brushing her hair. It was too long for this day and age, in my opinion, but it was the best looking thing about her. Her features were the kind that would look okay on someone older but had no particular school girl charm. "I'm going to have to wash this hair again today, you can just bet," she said, "because if there's one thing I can't stand . . ."

"Here comes Mom." I crammed the stuff back into the bag and held it out for Halcyon to drop in the brush. She took her time.

After much rearranging, we finally got most of the baggage into the trunk, but the big bag had to ride on the back seat with guess who crammed in beside it.

Halcyon, obviously an old pro at buttering up older people, suddenly went into an act. "It's so super magnificent of you, Mrs. Conrad, to take me in like this," she said.

Mom, trying to cut over to the outer lane, away from taxis and cars with opened trunks, could only murmur some polite nothing.

"I mean," Halcyon went on, "I'm touched. I really am, that you'd put yourself out for a strange girl like me."

Strange doesn't cut it, I thought. Try obnoxious. Offensive.

"My parents are grateful, and so am I," she said. "The Midwest is something I've always been curious

34

about, and here I am, right in the heart of it, thanks to you."

"The Midwest can get a little dull at times," Mom said. "Except for the weather, of course. It changes all the time."

"I love change!" Halcyon said, missing the point. "I love changing schools."

"Oh, really?" Mom surged ahead in the cleared lane. "Why is that, Halcyon?"

"It's more interesting, don't you think? Meeting new people all the time? Of course, I view things through the eye of a photographer."

"Is photography your hobby?" Mom asked.

"Hobby! It's my profession. Or at least it will be."

"That's interesting."

"My parents have a gallery, and one of these days I'm going to have a one-man show there."

Her use of the expression *one-man* grated on me.

"Did you take lots of photography courses?" Mom asked. "At the schools you've attended?"

"Schools! They didn't teach photography any place I've been. I've had a classical education."

"Well, that's wonderful," Mom said. "And so you've developed this . . . uh . . . profession all on your own?"

"You bet. And it hasn't been easy. I've had to fight, fight, fight for space to work in, and I got no encouragement from the faculty, not even the art department, when it came to showing my work. They're just so narrow."

"Harrison Junior High isn't classical," I said, just to get in on the conversation. "It doesn't even have much class, does it, Mom?"

"It's a very nice school," Mom said, with a warning glance in the rear-view mirror. "Well-rounded.

In fact, it's rated as one of the best suburban schools in the state."

"That's why I agreed to come out here," Halcyon said, looking straight forward. "I thought it was about time to broaden my scope. See what life is like for the average kid in the Midwest."

You fake, I thought. You came out here for no such reason. You're here because your folks couldn't afford to send you to private school and you couldn't come down to the level of the kids in your building. I could just see Halcyon lording it over them whenever she had the chance. But to come out here and live with strangers, just to save face! Boy, I'd never do such a thing. Of course, I was just an *average Midwest kid*.

I saw a difficult year stretching ahead. True, I had great plans, and true, Angel was going to help them come about. But *The Year of the Clara* didn't seem like such an arm-flinging thing any more. It might even call for a pair of boxing gloves.

SIX

As we left the tollway and drove the three miles into town, Mom rambled on to Halcyon about how the outlying areas were building up with shopping centers and housing developments. But our village itself has stayed pretty much the same (she wasn't just kidding), even though a lot of the people who now lived there commuted into the city every day.

Our house is only four blocks from what you could laughingly call the heart of the town, but it's almost like country. Maybe it's because the land going off from ours is low-lying and marshy, so no one wants to build out there. In fact, there's a weed-ringed pond down a little distance from our house and Jay Frank's.

"That's where we live, just ahead," Mom said, turning the corner. "The big white house."

"Oh," Halcyon said. "Two stories."

At least she didn't say, "How unimpressive," or "It looks like it needs some work."

After Halcyon glanced around for a bellboy who didn't materialize, we all struggled inside the house with the stuff. Halcyon and I did most of the struggling, because Mom, after carrying in two of the smaller bags, excused herself from the action. It was just natural with her. Mom's a mental mover, not a physical worker. At school she has trillions of kids at her beck and call to carry things around and run errands.

Halcyon, when she had to, could really move, and we had the stuff upstairs in no time. Before I knew what was happening, she was grabbing all of Laurel's boxes from the closet and dumping them into the hall. Then she eyed the furniture.

"You'll have to help me shift this bed to the other side," she said, in that bossy tone I'd already come to know. "And that chest goes over there."

"Actually, what's wrong with things the way they are now?"

"I want to be comfortable. *Okay?*"

Her *okay* translated to *what's wrong with YOU?*

It was obvious that, for some unknown reason, Halcyon had no intention of liking me. Feeling confused and guilty, I helped her rearrange the furniture.

Halcyon took a shower and shampooed her hair and was drying it when I went up to tell her lunch was ready.

"This will take a while," she said over the hum. "My hair is just so thick and long. I have to spend hours on it."

"Then do you mind if we go ahead? Mom has some errands."

"Be my guest," Halcyon said.

38

Words failed me, as they seldom do.

We did eat, and Mom went off. I had stuck the potato salad (from the deli section of the supermarket) and jello (same source) away and was wrapping the cheese and ham when Halcyon strolled into the room.

"I'll have some of that," she said.

I put it back onto the platter and was about to get out the rest of the stuff when I got a better idea. "Help yourself," I said. "Just put it back when you're finished. In this heat . . ."

"I meant to ask you about that, upstairs," Halcyon said, piling about three slices each of meat and cheese on bread. "What's wrong with the air-conditioning?"

"Nothing's wrong. We don't have any."

She stop-motioned. "I never heard of such a thing!"

"You have now."

"But it's hot up there!"

"It cools off at night. Some."

Halcyon bit into her sandwich. "Do you have any Pepsi around this place?"

"Just diet 7-Up."

"All right. I'll have some."

I just loved that *I'll have some* expression of hers and sooner or later I'd tell her so.

Although watching people eat is not one of my favorite pastimes, I sat there while Halcyon attacked the sandwich. I'd like to think it was to keep her company and try to make her feel welcome, but to be honest, I guess I was out to prove what a pleasant person I am.

"What was it like at boarding school?" I asked,

trying not to sound impressed, just interested. "Was it fun?"

Halcyon scooped some dripping mustard from the plate and smeared it back onto the sandwich. "Fun? To some kids, I guess you could call it that. The Looney Tunes crowd."

"What do you mean?"

"Oh, they carried on like crazy. Every week some new caper."

"Like what?"

Halcyon looked bored. "For one thing, they'd penny doors. You know what that is, don't you?" At my negative shake of the head, she said, "The doors to the dorm rooms opened out. Kids would wedge pennies on the outside, under the sills, and the girls couldn't get out. They'd have screaming fits."

It sounded kind of like fun to me. "What else?"

"They put vaseline on the toilet seats. Stuff like that. The faculty never knew about those things, but there was a big ruckus when a girl got caught putting a cigarette in the fingers of a statue, which just happened to be of the founder of the school."

I smiled, which was a bad move.

Halcyon finished off her drink and plopped down the glass. "Those guys kept the whole place in an uproar, so the serious ones, the ones with a *career* in mind, just couldn't get any place because of the commotion. And I was kept from moving around at night, the only free time I had to try to develop my film, because the staff wouldn't make any exceptions to the dorm rule." She got up and looked in the refrigerator. "Don't you have any more chilled 7-Up?"

"No. There's an eight-pack in that cupboard. You'll have to use ice."

Halcyon took a few ice cubes and dumped the rest in the sink to melt. She didn't put the cap back on the bottle.

I did it, and then said mildly, "We kind of save ice cubes because our refrigerator doesn't have an automatic ice-maker."

"Oh, don't be so bossy," Halcyon said. "Just because you live here."

Bossy? Me?

"Anyone home?" Jay Frank had his face against the screen door.

"Come on in," I called, burning at Halcyon's remark.

Jay Frank came in, looking shy, and I introduced him to Halcyon.

"Pull up a chair, stranger," Halcyon said. "Want me to make you a sandwich?"

"He's already eaten," I said.

"I've already eaten," Jay Frank told Halcyon.

"Then help me kill this bottle, no use letting it go to waste," she said, pouring the drink and taking out another tray of ice cubes.

"You're nice," Jay Frank said to Halcyon, after a glance at me.

"He usually drinks Hawaiian Punch," I said, giving him a look which he chose to ignore. "Did you want something special?" I asked. It was rude, I knew, and it wasn't fair to take out my general annoyance on Jay Frank, but the admiring look he was giving Halcyon really rankled. I mean, all the tender, loving care I'd showered on him all these years was going right down the chutes for a lousy glass of pop.

41

"I just wanted to meet your new sister," Jay Frank said.

Where had he heard that word? Had I actually used it in front of him?

"We're not sisters," Halcyon said, beating me to it. "Want to come up and help me put up my photos?"

Before I realized it, they were going upstairs and there I was left with the clean-up.

Okay, I thought, I'll do it this time, but there are going to be some rules laid out around here. As I was finishing, Jay Frank appeared and asked for a hammer and small nails.

"What for?"

"Halcyon needs them."

I took them up myself. Halcyon had framed photographs laid out in formation on the bed.

"You're not going to hang all those, are you?" I asked.

"No, dear, I'm going to stand here and hold them against the wall for the next few months."

The look I gave Jay Frank stopped his giggles. "You've got what, about twenty photos there?" I said to Halcyon. "I doubt if Mom wants that many holes in the plaster."

She hesitated, hammer in hand, then shrugged. "Come to think of it, I'd rather highlight one or two. Maybe I'll attach a light to shine onto them."

You do that, I thought.

"These are kind of funny pictures," Jay Frank said, studying them one by one. "No people."

"I deal in reality," Halcyon said. "Buildings and garbage cans and alleys *are* what they *are*."

You fake! I wanted to shout. I'll bet you don't

photograph people because you can't focus on them. You're so two-faced yourself. But all I said was, "See you guys later."

Halcyon didn't bother to answer as I left the room. But, then neither did Jay Frank. Creep! Traitor!

SEVEN

I THOUGHT MAYBE YOU'D BRING HALCYON ALONG," Angel said over at her house Tuesday afternoon. "I'm dying to meet her." She gave me a look. "Or are you two still not hitting it off?"

"Listen, I try. But she acts as though I'm just someone she has to put up with. Me!" I flopped onto Angel's bed. "Besides, she's always going off, taking those dumb pictures. Know where she is today?"

Angel, standing at her desk, glancing at some papers, asked, "Where?"

"Chicago."

"Chicago!" Angel gave me a surprised look. "Alone?"

I nodded. "On the train. Off she went, big as you please, camera slung on her shoulder. I doubt Mom even knows. She's off at school, getting ready for tomorrow."

"She sounds so sure of herself. Halcyon, I mean." Angel's tone had a hint of awe in it. But then, after a glance at me, she quickly added, "Still, there are limits. Your mother is a very patient person and understanding, but yet . . ."

"She can strike like a killer whale," I finished, "when pushed too far."

"Speaking of your mother," Angel said, coming over to the bed with one of the papers, "did you square it away with her? About the rat experiment? Fergy's assembling the materials, and we'd like to get started next week."

"Yeh, sure, it's okay." I guessed it was. That conversation with Mom seemed so long ago.

"Well, good." Angel handed me the paper. "Here's our sketch for the rat run. The process is quite simple. We place a rat here . . ."—she pointed— ". . . then raise a lever and see how long it takes him to race down to this point here to get the pellet of food."

"That's really fascinating," I said, bored out of my skull.

"Really. We'll do the run for several weeks, with variatons. Some days we'll withhold food, and then the next day check to see if the rat has lost interest."

I had lost all kinds of interest myself. Handing back the sketch, I said, "Just be sure the cellar doesn't smell. That's the main thing."

"It won't. Oh, Clara, those rats are so cute. We were looking at some the other day and I could hardly keep my hands off them."

"Have you seen Skip lately?" Now what kind of weird word association made me say that?

"As a matter of fact, yes." Angel sighed. "He's become such a bore."

"*Skip?*" There was a little squeak in my voice.

"Sports, sports, sports. I tried to lead him off into other subjects, like an article I just read about cloning, but do you know what? He said circus things are for kids. Can you actually believe that boy? He doesn't even read *Newsweek*."

"Athletes don't have time for current events."

"Ha! If Skip's an example, they have plenty of time to spend in front of a mirror. His blow-dryer must get a real workout."

"Angel, you sound so mean. You used to like him a lot last year."

"He's changed. Skip's become the Big Star. I don't go for that image."

I'd go for it. Impulsively, I asked, "Have you thought any more about Pom Pon? About how to get me on the squad?"

"I've taken the first steps." Angel put the sketch back on her desk. "Had a little talk with Miss Curry about my dropping out, and then I mentioned your name, how talented you are, what an asset you'd be, et cetera. Now it's up to you to work like a demon and not make me out a liar."

I suddenly felt rigid. "Angel, you know I can do cartwheels and splits . . . things like that . . . but when am I going to learn those special things you need to know for tryouts?"

"Right now. Let's go out in back."

Working in the yard, on grass, was not too good in a way, but at least when I fell I didn't break anything. As I'd said, I could do cartwheels . . . but six in a row? Angel just didn't let up for a minute.

"Now do two flips, a twirl, two more cartwheels, and then a split. And raise your arms and smile up at the crowd there at the last." She snapped her fingers. "Go!"

"Oh, hey, come on," I complained. "That's too much."

With hands on her hips, Angel said, "Nothing's too much when you've got a goal. Come on, get up and stop panting like a decrepit collie. You've got to prove you're better than any of the other tryouts. Not *as good as*. Better. And then . . ." She shrugged. "You're on. After all, fair is fair."

Although my face already felt on fire and sweat trickled down my cheeks and matted my hair, I did what Angel commanded. Over and over. The whole backyard began to tilt a little and sway as I went into a twirl, twist, and tumble routine.

"That's it for today," Angel finally said, with a glance at her watch. "You look good, Clara. Considering."

"Good!" I sprawled on the grass. "Angel, I'm a wreck. I'll never be able to keep up. Not in my condition."

"I told you! You've got to work! Get into shape. Then you'll smile and not even sweat. I know it isn't easy, Clara, but that's the way it has to be, if you want to earn the reward." She dropped down beside me. "You could compare it to the way Fergy and I have to shape those rats to make them go after *their* reward."

"I love your comparison." Sitting up, I mopped my face with the bottom of my T-shirt.

"You want to continue or not?" Angel's eyes, fixed on me, looked like scoops of sky. "You can make it, Clara. But it's up to you to decide if it's worth the effort."

I could see those bleachers full of admiring faces. Hear the band. See myself as the darling of the football-basketball team. I smiled. "Think I'll look good in the outfit?"

Angel smiled back. "Knockout. Pure knockout.

They'll have to put blinders on the guys to keep their minds on the game."

Not *him,* I thought. Let him look for all he's worth. But would Skip even notice me? After Angel? That was a far-out idea, even for a daydream.

"Hello there, you look as though you had a bad day," was the way Halcyon greeted Mom as she came dragging in around six that night.

"Bad doesn't begin to describe it," Mom said.

Halcyon leaped up from the kitchen table where she'd been fiddling around with her camera. "Here, let me take your briefcase." It was more of a satchel. "My, it's heavy."

"Loaded with work." Mom sat down. "It seems to get worse every year, or else I'm getting old."

"I guess you'll be retiring soon."

Mom looked up. "I'm not *that* old."

"Here's some iced tea," I said, handing Mom a glass. With Halcyon gone all day we still had plenty of ice cubes. "I put together some dinner, but it's not great."

"Thanks, honey. Anything will do."

"I'll just take this stuff upstairs and then set the table," Halcyon said. She was being unusually agreeable.

"No rush, unless you two are hungry. I'd like to put up my feet and relax for a few minutes." Picking up her glass, Mom headed for the lounger in the living room.

"I had a snack in the station, so don't rush on my account," Halcyon called.

"There's a letter from Laurel," I said, walking with Mom. "It's on the piano."

I handed her the envelope, but instead of looking

at it, Mom looked at me. "What did Halcyon mean, she had a snack in the station? What station?"

"I guess she meant in Chicago. She went in today to take photos."

Mom's breath hissed a little as she leaned forward with a jerk. "Halcyon!" As though on cue, Halcyon came into the room, carrying her camera. "Am I to understand," Mom said, "that you went into the city today? Alone?"

"That's right." Halcyon's tone was pleasant, without a trace of worry. In her case, I'd have been shaking in my shoes.

"Without even letting me know."

"The idea just came to me, and I took off." Halcyon ventured a smile. "Mrs. Conrad, you're probably just not used to girls who get ideas and act on them."

Mom was, I think, stunned into silence.

"There was no problem," Halcyon went on. "Chicago's simple to get around in. I took some shots in . . . what do you call it? The Loop? And then I hiked over to Lake Shore Drive and caught the sweep of buildings along the lake. But my best roll, I believe, will be the one from Belmont Harbor."

"You found your way up there?" Mom looked almost more astonished than angry. "To Belmont Harbor?"

"I caught a bus. And then coming back, I took a cab to the station. My mother says that as long as you have cab fare and a sense of direction you can get any place. And here I am."

After a pause, Mom said, "All right. It's done. But next time you get an idea, Halcyon, check with me before you act on it. If I'm at school, contact me, even if I'm in a meeting. Is that clear?"

"Okay." Halcyon gave me a glance I couldn't quite read. Then she turned and went upstairs.

Mom looked at me and I couldn't read her expression either. Abruptly, she leaned back, stretched out on the lounger and closed her eyes. She seemed almost to be fighting a smile, but maybe she was just gritting her teeth. Laurel's letter was lying in her lap, still unread.

I went back to the kitchen. Boy, if I'd tried a caper like taking off to Chicago . . . pow! But I guess if you have enough gall, like Halcyon, you can get by with anything in this world.

During the first part of the meal no one said very much. Halcyon was lying low, testing the atmosphere, and Mom looked as tired as before.

"Is the enrollment up again this year?" I asked, to break the silence.

"No, as a matter of fact, it's decreased. We've had to cut out one of the fourth grade classes in Randolph School so that makes the other two classes larger than we'd like. The teachers aren't very happy about it. There are other problems, but I guess they'll get ironed out eventually. They always do."

"What's my school called again?" Halcyon asked.

"Harrison Junior High," I told her. "It's the biggest one around. And the best. We won in the finals last year. Basketball."

"Oh, sports," Halcyon said with a near sneer.

I gave her a put-down look and turned to Mom. "What's new with Laurel?"

"Working hard. Delighted with Juilliard. Oh, and she's had several meetings with your parents, Halcyon, and it's all set for her to move in this weekend. She's pleased with the arrangements, and I must say

I'm happier knowing there is someone around to keep an eye on her."

To keep my sister from sounding like an infant, I added, "Laurel's so wrapped up in her music she doesn't know where she's at, most of the time."

"I admire her so much," Halcyon said. "She's like me, really dedicated to her work."

Again, what gall! As though there were any comparison! "My sister's going to be a real talent someday, isn't she, Mom?" Then, turning to Halcyon, I said, "Laurel was into music before I was even born." I was warming up. "In fact, when I came along, Mom and Dad let Laurel decide what to call me, and that's why I was named Clara. After the girl in the *Nutcracker* ballet."

"You were not! You weren't named after her!"

I stared at Halcyon, speechless.

"You were named after Clara Schumann, the pianist."

This was so incredible I was at a loss. I looked at Mom for support. She picked up the iced tea pitcher, filled my glass, and gave me a glance. "Halcyon may be right. It sounds possible. I don't remember."

"I know I'm right!" Halcyon said. "Laurel told me herself. I mentioned to her that *Clara* was an old-fashioned kind of name and she told me this Schumann person was her ideal at the time. How did you get your name, Mrs. Conrad? *Jessie?*"

"That story has been lost to the ages," Mom said. "And it's just as well."

Mom retired to the desk in her room after dinner, leaving Halcyon and me to clean up the kitchen.

Halcyon must have sensed, from my short answers, and the way I slammed things around, that

I wasn't too thrilled with her conversation at dinner, but she didn't let on. "Tell me about the kids at school," she said, putting things away. "Are they cut-ups or serious?"

"Some of each."

"Do you have any best friends?"

I told her about Angel whom I'm sure I'd mentioned before, and this time really laid it on thick. She was the prettiest, the smartest, the most everything (true, of course) that ever came down the pike. "We've been friends since kindergarten," I finished, "and always will be."

"That's okay, if you like being that close to one person," Halcyon said. "I guess I'm too independent. Besides, I'd never let friends or the social scene get in the way of my work. My *photography*," she added, as though I didn't know.

"I think there's a camera club that meets after school," I said. "But as far as a darkroom . . ."

"Forget it! I'm planning on setting up my own. Here."

"Here? Where?"

As though she'd rehearsed it in her mind, Halcyon walked to the bathroom, just off the kitchen, and turned on the light. "This would do fine. I could cover up that window."

"Hey, you can't do that! This is Mom's. She moved her stuff down here and redecorated after Laurel and I more or less took over the bathroom upstairs. So don't think that now . . ."

"Oh, all right." Halcyon jabbed off the light. "But there must be another water source somewhere. This kitchen's too open. How about in the basement?"

"There's no water except in the laundry room.

But you wouldn't like it in there. It's so dreary, with no windows or . . ."

"No windows?" Halcyon's eyes widened. "Dark? Faucets?"

She was too much! "No. There's a stream running through, and we pound the clothes on the rocks."

"Which way is it?" Halcyon was already flicking on the stairway switch and clomping downstairs.

"That room to your left," I said, following. Wow, she'd gross out when she saw that room.

But Halcyon was enchanted. Looking around, she said, "Do you think I could develop down here when it's not being used for laundry?" A little pulse fluttered at the base of her throat.

"Ask Mom." I left, and Halcyon followed. "I'm sure she won't care, so long as you clean up and don't mess up the laundry. She likes for kids to have hobbies."

Wrong word. "I told you before, it's more than a hobby with me," Halcyon snapped. She stopped abruptly at the foot of the stairs and surveyed the larger room. "This will be okay, too," she said. "I can string up some wires and clip the prints onto them to dry." She took a step up and paused. "In fact, I might just set up a work table in this area, for cutting and trimming and mounting."

"Be my guest," I said.

Upstairs, we watched TV for a while and ate a bunch of junk. Then, feeling guilty because of my diet lapse (Angel had told me what foods to eat and what to avoid for high energy), I decided to go to the backyard and work out in the moonlight. Halcyon was by now hogging the bathroom anyway, with her big shampoo routine.

My muscles ached, but I worked out the pain. The things Angel had taught me seemed easier this time around. The combination of her strict coaching and my determination would truly turn the tide. This would be The Year of the Clara for sure!

And then the thought hit so hard I fell right out of a cartwheel and landed on one knee. Where had my mind been at, earlier, when I'd blithely told Halcyon she could use the cellar? The cellar had been promised. Promised for the high art of rat-shaping.

I drew up my knees to my chin, kissed the bruised one, and pondered on the ironies of life. Here was one cellar, dark, dingy, and neglected for years. And now suddenly it had become the Most Wanted Place for two parties, both with purpose and determination.

Fair is fair. Angel's words filtered into my mind.

Absolutely. She'd asked first, I'd known her longer, she was already into a school project. There were all kinds of reasons why Angel and the rats should win over Halcyon and her photography.

I'd just have to break the *no developing* news to Halcyon. I'd rather be whipped. Tomorrow would be soon enough to tell her. Or the next day. Whichever came first.

EIGHT

"ARE YOU ABOUT READY?" I ASKED HALCYON THE
next morning. "I'd like to get to school early."

"So, go," she said.

I shrugged and left. It was okay by me. I didn't
need Halcyon hanging like an albatross around my
neck. It was sort of unsettling, though, to think she
didn't want to be associated with me, either. I mean,
what had I done?

"Where's your girl friend?" Angel asked, as I
joined her on the front steps of the school. "I was
looking forward to meeting her at last."

"She's not my girl friend, and once you meet her
you'll wish you hadn't."

Angel squeezed my arm. "Come on, Clara. She
couldn't be that bad. Listen, I just saw Fergy and
it's all set for this coming weekend. That's one good
thing about starting school in the middle of the week.
Saturday comes so soon."

"Angel. About the cellar. There's something I
ought to . . ."

"You look different," she blurted. "Oh." The tiny frown smoothed. "You've fixed your hair a new way. It's darling. And your eyes . . ."

I shrugged. "I was just trying to copy the look of a magazine model. Is it too much?"

"Oh, no. I love it. Clara . . . ?" She gave a little laugh. "You don't have to blush. It's just me."

But it wasn't. Off in the distance, walking toward us was Skip Svoboda. "I'll meet you here after school," I said. The thought of seeing Skip up close, after I'd purposely planned for it, gave me stage fright. "Wait for me," I said over my shoulder.

"What were you going to say about the cellar?" Angel called.

"Tell you later." Later would be soon enough.

But after school, just as I met Angel, Halcyon came along. I introduced them, and we stood around for a while comparing classes. Naturally the subject of Skip didn't come up. I wondered if Angel had stayed to talk to him in the morning. I hadn't seen him again all day. The subject of the cellar didn't come up, either. I knew I should mention it while the two contenders were there together, but I just didn't. In some ways I'm quite the coward.

As Halcyon and I walked home, I asked her what she thought of Angel.

"Sweet kid."

"Sweet, yes, but not weak." Just a little advance warning there. I knew I should go on to warn Halcyon that she'd have to change her plans about using the cellar, but I didn't. I just hoped I wouldn't be around when she finally found out.

As a matter of fact, I wasn't. Around, I mean. I was over at Jay Frank's that Saturday, hearing how he had managed the last couple of days in the twilight time before Sheri got home. So far, so good. But Jay Frank must have been staying awake nights, thinking up possible crisis situations.

For example: "What if I'm making a milkshake and the blender breaks?" *"Clean up the mess, kid."*

"What should I do if someone calls and asks if I'm home alone?" *"Lie. Oh, Jay Frank, just tell them your mother can't come to the phone, she's busy. She is busy, you know, unless she goofs off at work."*

"What if I find a spider in the bathtub?" *"Make friends with it, or else turn on the shower,"* I sighed. "Could we just concentrate on the vital stuff? You're sure you know how to dial for fire, police, paramedics?" We'd only gone through the routine about ten thousand times.

"I know, I know. But if something happens, couldn't I just call you first?"

I felt like pounding my head against the wall. "How many times do I have to tell you I'll be staying after school most nights? That is, if I make Pom Pon."

"Maybe you won't." Jay Frank wrapped his thin arms around his chest.

"Oh, great. You're a real morale-builder. Why don't you just pay attention to what I'm telling you instead of putting me down?"

"I *am* paying attention," he said. "I know what to do. Only . . ."

"Only what?"

"I don't know what to do when nothing happens." He gave me a look from those hazelnut eyes. "I can't play games alone, and Sheri says I can't have friends over when she's not here."

I was getting irritated. "Read. Watch TV. Do your

homework. Find a hobby. You can't hang onto other people all your life."

"All right," he said softly.

"I've got to go home now," I said, turning away to keep myself from weakening and reaching out to him. "Angel and Fergy are coming over to set up the rat run, and I should be there to back them up when Halcyon throws the big fit."

"Fit?"

"She's going to blow her stack. I should have told her, but I didn't quite get around to it. There may be blood spilled before the afternoon is over."

"Well, you know how to dial the paramedics."

Cute kid.

I could hear pounding from the lower depths as I let myself into the kitchen, so I clipped downstairs, wondering how long Angel and Fergy had been there and how come they hadn't fetched me from next door, since I'd left a note outside.

"Hi," Angel greeted me, winging back her bangs. "Halcyon let us in, so we thought we'd just get started. How does it look so far?"

"Great," I said, glancing at what looked like nothing much at all. "Hi there, Fergy."

He waved at me with the hammer and went back to pounding nails.

To Angel, against the noise, I said, "I didn't know Halcyon would be back from her errands so soon. Did she throw a big scene?" The pounding stopped and those last words came out as a shout. Halcyon also came out . . . of the laundry room. I felt like crawling.

"You're back," she said brightly. "Everyone's been getting organized while you were away. I've got more of the stuff I'll need and I'm setting up . . ."

"But . . ." I looked toward the laundry room, at the rat-run-to-be, at Angel, and then at Halcyon. No sign of fits or fireworks.

"Isn't it great that we'll all be working down here together?" Halcyon went on, with an admiring look at Angel. "It'll be like a cooperative lab."

"What do you mean?" I couldn't quite take it all in.

"We've got it all planned," Halcyon said, looking smug and triumphant. "We'll work down here together. Angel and Fergy and I."

Angel and Fergy and I.

I should have felt relief. Instead, I felt like a shut-out in my own home. After a weak smile, I turned abruptly and hurried upstairs.

I thought Angel might come up, too. But she didn't.

"I'm glad you guys got together on your plans," I said, as I paused to catch my breath after my workout over at Angel's that night. "But I think I should warn you . . ."

Angel nodded. "Halcyon's probably no fun to live with. You would know that better than I would. But . . ."

"Yes?"

"But she's trying to get along."

"Meaning that I'm not?"

"Oh, Clara, you're the easiest person to get along with that I know. You've just got to be firm with that girl and not let her walk all over you. She'll respect you for it, believe me."

"As you said, you don't have to live with her."

Instead of answering, Angel started pulling off her clothes to take a shower.

"I'll leave as soon as my muscles unknot," I said, too pooped to move.

"That's okay." In bra and pants, Angel laid out her clothes for the next day. On top of the heap she put pink underpants with *Sunday* embroidered on the side. She was wearing *Saturday*.

"What would happen if one of those wore out or got lost in the laundry?" I asked.

Angel smiled. "I have spares, of course."

"Of course." I got to my feet. "In your book there's no such thing as chance. I wish I could lock into that system."

"It's no fat deal. Just advance planning. That's the way things work. Just like my coaching and slipping you the tricks of the trade is going to land you on Pom Pon. You'll see."

I saw all right, and it was just as Angel said. In the third week of school, when tryouts for Pom Pon finally took place, I got up when it was my turn and gave, if I may say so, a stunning performance. Actually, I imagined myself as Angel, going through the routines the way she had demonstrated them to me with flair and poise. It paid off. I felt keyed up as I went back to the group. Miss Curry was making lots of notes and some of the girls glared, so from that I knew I'd been good.

The next day, when the winners were posted, I tore down the hall and found Angel. "I made it! Hey, I made it!"

"Super! I'm so glad! Oh, Clara, you're going to be sensational!" She gave me a hug. "I just love your enthusiasm. That special spark is the best thing you've got going for you, other than your looks, of course."

"My looks? Since when have I had looks?"

She laughed. "You always have had. You know that. But now you're on the way to becoming a knockout. Don't pretend you haven't noticed, when everyone else has."

"Like who?"

Angel flung out her arms. "Should I make a list?"

"Cut it out." I could feel myself blushing again. There was only one name I truly cared about, and for all I knew, he was still enthralled by Angel.

I hung around the house and called a few kids who had also made the squad. When Halcyon got home, I told her the news.

"I guess that's considered hot stuff in the boonies, huh?" she said, digging into the refrigerator as usual. "Want to split this last piece of pie?"

"No, thanks. I'm surprised someone in your crowd didn't see the notice and mention it to you."

Halcyon gave me a look. "Why would they care? That Pom Pon jazz went out with the fifties. I'm just glad there are a few kids around the school who know where they're at."

I was burning. "If you mean your new friends, they're nowhere. Just drudges. Out for grades, and that's it."

"Not true! They're very interested in my *work*."

With a shrug, I murmured, "To each his own."

Halcyon snatched up her plate, scraped and rinsed it, and went upstairs. She claimed assignments here in the Midwest were simple compared to what she was used to in boarding school, but I noticed she studied every night without fail.

I thought Mom, at least, would swell with motherly pride over the Pom Pon news when we were alone after dinner, but she took it as a matter of course.

"Wasn't that the general idea, to get on the squad?" she asked. She took hold of my arm. "Good heavens, look at the size of that bruise!"

I jerked away. "Mom, you don't seem to realize . . . the competition!"

"I guess not." She smiled. "But give me a break, will you? This is all so new to me."

And you look so tired, I thought. I hugged her. "It's just that this is the beginning . . ."

"Of what?"

"Of everything!"

"Oh, Clara. I am happy for you. Really. Congratulations." She kissed me. Then, with a sigh, she pulled away. "On to paper work. The everlasting paper work."

"I've got homework, too." I pushed a gray hairpin back into one of Mom's braids and gave it a pat. "See you."

But upstairs, instead of studying my lessons I studied myself in the full-length mirror. Looks. Did I have looks? Angel should know, although her own meant little to her.

But looks didn't necessarily lead to popularity. If I was going to make this my all-out year I'd have to tag every base.

Angel had her *future* list. I'd have my *present*.

Grabbing a sheet of paper, I headed it POPULARITY MUSTS. That stopped me for a while, but finally I came up with the following:

POPULARITY MUSTS

1. Be as cute looking as possible
2. Get on Pom Pon (done)
3. Hang out with the right crowd

4. Go out with the cutest guy possible
   (!!!!!!)
5. Get invited to parties
6. Keep in fashion (Needs work)
7. Keep up grades   (" ")
8. Be friendly with *everyone*

There came a sudden pounding of hoofs and Halcyon dashed into my room.

"What do you want?" Why couldn't she learn to knock before barging in?

"Here are some proofs, close-up shots of one of the rats downstairs. This one's Little Blue."

"Who?"

"You know. I told you they put dye marks on the rats' foreheads to tell them apart. Isn't he a sweetie?"

Halcyon stuck one of the ugliest photos I'd ever seen in front of me. "Don't touch it," she said, "it's still damp. I just thought you'd like a preview."

"It's revolting," I said, walking over to my closet.

"Huh! Well, you can just bet . . ."

I checked through a few shirts and then, wondering at the silence, turned around. Halcyon was reading my list. "I can't believe this," she said.

"Give me that!" I raced over and snatched the paper from her hand. "You've no right . . . !"

With a smile that was almost a smirk she left the room.

I slammed the door after her and then yanked open a desk drawer and shoved my list under a pile of old spiral notebooks. I felt as though Halcyon had seen me naked or something. It was worse, in a way. She had seen my bare thoughts.

Gritting my teeth, I vowed not to let it worry me. I didn't care what Halcyon thought. She'd had a low opinion of me from the moment we met, for no reason, and she'd made no effort to try to understand me.

I got out my books and turned to the English lit assignment.

The truth was, I didn't understand Halcyon, either. And a further truth was that I didn't intend to try.

NINE

IT ENTERED MY MIND THAT HALCYON MIGHT TELL her special group about my popularity plan, but in the next couple of days the drudges I happened to meet didn't react in any way. So I guess Halcyon either forgot about the list or considered it beneath mention. At least I could be glad she didn't stoop to gossip.

But other kids, because of Pom Pon, did begin to notice me. As if by magic, I had suddenly become *someone* at Harrison Junior High. Girls I didn't even know all that well started saying, "Hi, Clara!" in the halls, and some of the guys began hanging around. True, most of the things they said were put-down kidding remarks—that's par for the course in eighth grade. The really big thing, though, was that the other girls on the First Squad started being friendly.

Liz Halston, for example, who had never talked to me before unless I was with Angel, rushed up one day in the hall and smiled as though I was her closest friend. "The group's getting together at my house Friday night," she said. "Bring along practice clothes because we want to get that pregame routine down pat. Oh, and bring money, too," she said, giving a little wave as she pulled away to go down a side corridor.

"Money?"

"For send-outs," she called. "Chow-chow."

"Oh. Sure!"

As Liz faded away so did my smile. Money. How much? And was this a routine thing?

I didn't have much money at my fingertips. Mom gave me an allowance for helping around the house, but it didn't go very far. She'd always made me deposit the Jay Frank baby-sitting money in my savings account. I'd probably have to ask her to increase my allowance or else try to talk her into letting me withdraw some money. Neither idea appealed.

I was still standing in the hall, mulling over the situation when a hand slipped along the back of my neck, like a strangler casing the territory. I jumped a mile.

"Hey, relax," a voice said.

I twisted around and almost passed out on the spot because there I was, face to face with Skip . . . Skip Svoboda! "Oh, hi," I said. I wondered if he could feel the goose bumps.

"Hi, yourself." Whenever I'd seen Skip up this close before, Angel had been beside him. Had he grown even handsomer during the summer, or was it just a new hair styling plus rugged maturity? I felt weak.

His eyes, the color of blue jeans, looked down into mine. (Skip, naturally, is tall.) "Hear you made

Pom Pon," he said, with a smile that was teasing and a voice husky with undertones.

"Yeh. Who told you? Angel?" Why did I have to say that?

He gave a little negative shrug. "The guys keep track." For another moment his look locked with mine. Then, abruptly, he was off.

I sagged against the wall. What did it mean? *Everything?* Had—but this was unbelievable—had Angel honestly meant that she was through with Skip? And was she in fact turning him over to me? But that, of course, was impossible. Skip Svoboda was his own man. He could have any girl in Harrison Junior High as a steady.

Naturally, I didn't even mention Skip at the party Friday night, but I certainly tuned in when the girls started talking about the team members. It didn't seem to matter if a guy was a no-show in the looks department or if he had the personality of a fig. If he played on the first team, he was up for grabs.

Liz Halston's house is in a really plush neighborhood. We had the whole recreation room downstairs to work in, once we'd pushed the Ping-Pong table to the side. There was even a soda fountain built into the bar, but there was nothing in it. Liz passed out a few soft drinks and then said she was ready to take orders for pizza. "Just don't forget, you guys," she told us, "you've got to throw in for a tip, too. I mean, the kid is delivering and we live out a-ways."

"We ought to meet at houses closer into town from now on," Beth Anne Meyers said. "I'd offer my place, but we don't have a big enough room to practice in. How about you, Erica?"

"Okay. We have a big basement."

"Mindy?"

"Yeh. How about you, Clara?"

"I . . . uh. We just have a cellar. It wouldn't be any good. Besides, Angel and Fergy are using it for a science project."

"Isn't that girl—Halcyon—using it, too?" Mindy asked. "I heard her carrying on about her photography in the cafeteria the other day." Mindy made a face. "She brags a lot, doesn't she?"

Liz walked over. "How come she's living with you, anyway, Clara?"

Before I could answer, Leanne butted in. "Don't you know? She got kicked out of some swank boarding school because of wild pranks. The school insisted she apologize, but her folks wouldn't let her and yanked her out instead. I think it's awful, Clara, that you got stuck with her just because she's a friend of the family."

I shrugged. "We go our own ways." I'd had no idea Halcyon had been telling a story like that, but as little as I liked her, I wasn't going to blow her act. She hadn't blabbed about my popularity list, so in turn I'd keep quiet about her family's money problems. As Angel had pointed out, fair is fair.

"Really," Liz said, sweeping her hair to the side, "who cares about that girl and her snob school anyway? Let's practice while we wait for the pizza. Some of us really need to sharpen up." She didn't look at me.

We made a little progress, but I could see it wasn't going to be easy. Every night after school we worked out. Even after a month my muscles still ached the next morning.

Sometimes when Miss Curry made us go over and over a routine, or when some of us had to sit on the sidelines, bored out of our skulls while one or two worked to get the moves, I'd wonder why I'd ever let myself in for this punishment. The promise was there . . . the big show-off time at the games . . . but sometimes it seemed the promise would never take place. Work and wait. Work and wait. And there was always criticism. If not from Miss Curry, from the girls themselves, who had fallen into complaints and insults. I felt let-down.

In the meantime, now that I wasn't home after school, wouldn't you know that all kinds of things were going on there? Not great things, to my way of thinking, but there was a kind of loop-the-loop excitement in the air.

One night in October when I got home early I went down to the cellar to check out the action. The run was set up and there were cages lining one wall. Angel greeted me with "Purple did it in point six three seconds! Some kind of record!"

"Thrilling."

"Isn't it!" She brushed back her hair and turned to Fergy. "Would he do it again, do you think, for Clara?"

"I don't know." Fergy resettled the canvas hat on his head. He looked like a proud parent, torn between a natural desire to show off his prodigy and a concern for its health.

"Don't put a strain on Little Purple's heart. Not on my account," I said. "I have to live with myself, remember."

"You're putting us on," Angel, who is nobody's fool, observed. "But that's all right. I'd rather you did that than have you pretend something you don't feel."

"Yeh," Fergy said. "The real feeling comes from working with these animals every day and getting top performance out of them. We're about ready to go into phase two."

"What's that?" I asked.

"They're onto the reward system, which is sprinting down the runway for food," Fergy said. "Now they've gotta learn to reach out for it."

"Reach out where?"

"See this little lever?" Fergy moved to the end of the run with me following. "I just finished setting it up. At first, when the subject comes near to it, he gets a food pellet."

Angel, hovering close by, added, "We have no idea how long it will take to sink into their skulls . . . the idea of reward, I mean. But once it does, we move on to the next phase. They have to put a paw on the *lever* to release the food!"

"I want to be here for that one," I said. "Sounds like a real biggie."

Fergy pulled at the sides of his hat. "We'll let you know, if you shape up your attitude."

"Shape up your rats and let me worry about my attitude. I suppose you'll notify the wire services, the networks, maybe even NASA when Little Blue or Little Purple or whoever first puts his tiny paw on the lever?"

"Not quite. We go another step farther." Fergy cleared his throat. "After the subject learns to put a paw on the lever, he has to *press* it!"

Dead silence. Then, "That's it? He learns to press the lever?"

They nodded. Angel looked radiant.

"What would happen," I asked, "if your so-called subjects pressed the lever and surprise, surprise—no pellet?"

Fergy looked solemn. "If that happened often enough, they'd lose interest."

Like I'm doing right now, I thought. At that moment my attention was drawn to a line strung across the room with another batch of disgusting rat photos attached. "Can't Halcyon find something else to photograph?" I asked. "Not that I want to put down your little friends, but there is, after all, a whole world of other things out there."

"Maybe you could suggest that to her," Angel said to Fergy. "I have the feeling she's making our rats nervous with that flash. Little Red was edgy yesterday, didn't you think? What was his time, again?"

I left them muttering over their charts and headed upstairs. I tossed my sweater onto a kitchen chair and looked in the refrigerator for a quick snack. There'd been a couple of peaches yesterday, but they were gone. We'd made a poor economic exchange between Laurel, the food-untouchable, and Halcyon, the human disposal. I lifted the milk carton but it lapped with the weight of about an inch. That glutton! We'd had a full quart this morning. I slammed the door shut.

I was thinking of running out to the store or making Halcyon go when someone rang the back doorbell. Jay Frank scuttled inside. He stopped when he sighted me. "Hey, Clara, how come you're home?"

"They canceled practice because of a teachers' meeting. How are you, kid?"

"Fine." He was hugging a book to his chest.

"You lose your key?"

"Nope." He fished it out on its chain.

"How are you getting along?" He looked okay. Thin as always, but he didn't have the forlorn look I sort of expected, and tried to avoid seeing.

"I have a new friend," he said. "Besides Angel and Fergy and Halcyon."

His saying those names cut through to me a little. I focused on the other. "Who's your new friend? Does he live near here?"

"So far I can't figure out where he lives." Jay Frank slid sideways onto a chair, still clutching the book. His sneaker laces, in spite of all my training, still dangled, untied.

"Why won't he tell you where he lives?"

Jay Frank looked at me as though I'd lost my marbles. "Because raccoons can't talk."

Oh, no! Not another member of the animal kingdom. "You have a raccoon for a friend, huh?"

"Yes, and I'm learning all about him." Jay Frank laid the book on the table. "Fergy loaned this to me. So now I know it's either a hollow log or a culvert."

"What is?"

"Where he lives! What do you think!"

I didn't care much for Jay Frank's tone, or for the conversation in general. "So go crawl into a log or into a culvert," I muttered.

"I guess I could just follow Racky home some night after I feed him. After he gets tamer."

"Racky. Is that what you call him? That's really original."

"His real name is Rac. I just call him Racky for short."

I ripped a sheet of paper from the telephone pad and handed it to Jay Frank along with a ballpoint. "Write *Racky*. R-a-c-k-y."

He printed it, his fingertips whitening with the effort.

"Now write *Rac*. R-a-c."

He did.

72

"Okay, look at them. How can *Racky* be short for *Rac* when it has more letters?"

With lips pressed together, Jay Frank gave me an I-hate-you look. Then he threw the pen across the room, grabbed his book, and ran out the door.

I stood there looking at the pen, and then I went over and picked it up. Why had I deliberately done that to Jay Frank?

I didn't know why, and I didn't want to think about it. I took a couple of dollars out of the spare money jar and went out to buy some milk.

TEN

ALL DURING DINNER HALCYON CARRIED ON A
nonstop monologue about the Great Rat Experiment. "This is only a demonstration, what we're
doing," she said. (Since when was it a "we"?) "Did
you know, Mrs. Conrad, that even the lowest forms
of life can be trained? Like inchworms . . ." She
looped up a limp slice of fried onion. "Inchworms
can be trained to avoid light."

Thrills, chills and excitement. "I'll clear up," I
said, pushing away from the table. What with the
rat and worm topics, I'd had it.

When Mom finished her coffee, she said, "Halcyon, how would you like to show me what you're
doing downstairs?" I don't think she meant for her
voice to sound like an indulgent parent's at Kindergarten Open House, but that's the way it came
through to me. She paused. "Clara, I'm expecting a
call from Mr. Stein, a teacher, so be sure to let me
know."

I was doing the electric skillet when the phone

rang. I had to dry my hands before I could grab the receiver and say, "Mrs. Conrad's residence."

"My, how formal. Hi, there."

My heart zinged like a rubber ball on elastic. Then it pinged back into place. "Uh . . . hi."

"Skip Svoboda."

I *knew*. Who else had a voice like that? "Oh. Hi." (Don't sound too eager, Clara. But don't sound dull.) "How are you?"

"Great. The reason I'm calling . . ."

I clutched the counter and willed my voice to sound calm. "Yeh, why are you calling?" A little laugh there, keep it light.

"I'm calling because some of us guys were wondering, nothing special you know, but kind of wondering who was up for captain of Pom Pon this year."

"Oh?" What a big deal thing to call about. "I don't know. Miss Curry said there's no hurry. We should get to know the routines first and . . ."

"Yeh, I heard she's that way. You've gotta give her a nudge. Our team took care of election first week."

"I guess you're captain, huh?" Brilliant. Everyone knew Skip was captain. I hurried on with, "You're right, we should get at it, the games are about to start. Have you talked to Liz, too?"

"No way. You can handle it." His soft, easy tone made my heart go *ping* again. What was the meaning of this conversation? I felt flattered and confused.

"Well . . ." was all I could manage.

"Well, that's about it," Skip said. "Just thought I'd see if you could hurry things along."

"I'll try . . ." (But why?)

"You'd better," he said with a gentle laugh. Then, "You're real cute, Clara."

"Wh . . . what?"

Again the little laugh. Was I imagining, or was it affectionate? "I'd rather repeat it in person. See you. S'long."

Hanging up, I was practically at point pass-out, but the sound of Mom's footsteps snapped me back.

"Didn't the phone ring? Why didn't you call me?"

"It was for me." I stood there, palms on the counter.

"Clara? Is something wrong?"

"No." I turned. Thank goodness Halcyon had stayed downstairs. "That was Skip. Skip Svoboda." Just saying his name did something to me.

"Oh, yes." Mom made the familiar gesture of re-anchoring a hairpin in her braid. "Where have I heard that name?"

"Mom, he's only our star basketball player, and not bad on the football field either. He even had his picture in the paper once."

"Ummm." She was trying, but still came up a blank.

"Mom . . . don't you remember, Angel used to go out with him? I mean, they used to pair off at pep rallies and after-game parties and school things like that. She talked to you about him. I know she did."

"Now I remember." She started from the room and paused. "Did you say Angel *used* to go out with him?"

"Yeh." Why did I feel so funny? "I guess so."

Mom glanced at her watch. "I'm going to watch that *Medieval Castles* rerun on TV, but I'll probably hear the phone. Clara?"

I looked at her and she looked at me.

"Never mind." She shook away the thought. "Nothing."

I felt relieved that whatever it was, she hadn't said it. I didn't want anything to dim the glow. *You're real cute, Clara.* Skip had actually said that. I felt weak all over again.

There's something about being in a state of bliss that cocoons you from annoyances. That evening, unable to settle down to studying and too restless to stay in my room, I actually accepted Halcyon's invitation to come into her room and help her select rat photos for a future *definitive exhibition,* as only she would put it.

"Where are you going to show them?" I asked, taking in the glossies spread across her bed, dresser, and desk and being surprised that the basic repulsiveness of them didn't even get to me on this night.

"It depends." She picked up two photos that looked identical and chose one. "This is the better, don't you think?"

"For sure. What are you going to shoot next?"

"I may move on to humans. With them I could probably get more variety of expression."

A quick look showed that she was serious. I paused, then said, "Would you take my picture some time?"

"Why?"

I felt flustered. What *was* the deep, hidden reason? *Gary carried Mindy's picture in his wallet.* If Skip . . . oh, he wouldn't . . . but if . . .

Halcyon was studying my face as though I were some object. "I might use you for practice," she said after a bit, "but I can't promise you any prints."

"Why not?"

77

"It depends on how they turn out. I wouldn't want any inferior work floating to the surface after I become famous."

I heaved a sigh. "Forget it, Halcyon. Just forget it."

She gathered up her prints. "All right, I will. I'll be looking for people with character in their faces anyway. Like bums, streetwalkers . . ."

I should have been offended, I guess, but for some reason as I left Halcyon in her room, I felt sorry for her. She was so far out she wasn't even in the game.

The next morning I got up early to put in extra time on looking knock-out, but I didn't see Skip once.

He was so much on my mind, though, that I just had to mention his name when Angel and I were having lunch. She didn't react, so that gave me the courage to tell her he had called me last night.

"Oh, I'm glad." She actually did look pleased. "I hope you two can get together. That is, if you want to."

If I want to! Sometimes I couldn't believe Angel. "Isn't that up to him?" I said, with a shrug.

"Clara! You can have any guy you like. You should know that."

I didn't know it. But I did know one thing. I wanted Skip Svoboda and now, with Angel pulling herself out of the running . . . maybe I had a chance. But there was no way of knowing for sure. Not yet.

A low blow was handed out at Pom Pon practice after school.

"The orders got mixed up a little," Miss Curry

said, "but the outfits have finally arrived. As with all things, the prices have gone up this year, but we're stuck with the same school budget. So you girls are going to have to make up the difference in cost."

There were a few faces that showed concern, but not to the degree I was feeling.

"The show pom pons, the vinyl ones, are covered by the budget, of course," Miss Curry went on. "But I'll have to ask you girls to pay for the practice ones yourself. They're made of paper, as you know, and get pretty beat up. But each pair you buy should last a few weeks, if you're careful."

"When should we bring the money?" Erica asked.

"Next practice, if possible. I'll give you the charge slips later. Now girls, I want you to line up for the march formation. Frankly, I'm not impressed with what you've been doing so far, and if you don't get it together mighty fast I might just pull you out of the parade next week."

There was a lot of grousing around because no one particularly liked marching. It was tough to do the steps and still stay in formation.

"I thought we were going to elect our captain today," Liz Halston said, pulling her famous injured expression. "You said we would."

"I said *soon*." Miss Curry started handing out the paper pom pons. "You won't need a captain if you don't get the march formation down pat today. Let's get started, and later, if there's time, you can try on the outfits."

"I wish she'd retire," Liz muttered. "All she cares about is *show*."

"And all you care about is being elected captain," Mindy said. "For all the good it will do you."

"What's that supposed to mean?"

"Girls!" Miss Curry came over with a handful of pom pons. "Could we please get going?"

The practice went fairly well, and later we did get to try on the crimson pullovers with their white accent bands and the short pleated skirts that showed white inside pleats when we twirled.

Me—Clara Conrad—decked out in the official Pom Pon outfit! I could hardly believe it was real. The snuggly, covered-up feeling of the top . . . then the short, fluttery skirt . . . and then the long, cool stretch of bare legs down to the socks and sneakers just about knocked me out. It made play costumes, Halloween get-ups, new holiday outfits just nothing by comparison.

Liz Halston's voice came through to me. "I really think, Miss Curry, we should have the election. We're late this year as it is, and you may know that the boys . . ."

Miss Curry looked up from her check list, ran a hand through her hair, and with a sigh said, "Oh, go ahead. Here's some paper, Liz. Tear it up ballot size and everyone write down the name of the girl you want for a leader."

"Should we vote for co-captain, too?" Leanne, the only other new girl besides me and the alternates, asked.

"No, the runner-up will be co-captain."

I stood with my ballot, not knowing what name to put down. Liz? She seemed the obvious choice, now that Angel had dropped out.

Mindy sidled up to me. "You can vote for yourself," she said in an undertone.

"Me?"

"You'd better. My boyfriend Gary said . . ."

"Could we cut the chatter and just get this over

with?" Miss Curry said. "The custodian will be around . . ."

I quickly scribbled Mindy's name on the slip and handed it to Miss Curry.

"Leanne," she said, "please write each name I call out on that blackboard, and put a mark for each vote."

Judging by the rapt faces of the girls and the little darting glances, I could see this was more than a mere choosing of captain. There was an undercurrent of something, but I couldn't figure out what.

Liz's name was called out. And then again. Then mine.

Mine! Mindy, probably. But then my name was called again and again. Five times in a row. I felt sort of suspended. No one looked anywhere but at the blackboard, except me.

Mindy's name went up. Whew. Then Liz's.

Mine. Several times in a row. Then Erica's. The girl next to her said something, probably, "You did it," because Erica blushed.

When the last slip was read, my name had the most marks behind it, and then Liz's.

"That's that," Miss Curry said, spilling the slips into a wastebasket. "Congratulations, Clara and Liz. You'll have to work extra hard."

Liz wouldn't look at me, but from the glances of some of the other girls, huddling around her, you'd think I'd rigged the election.

"Tough toenails for Liz," Mindy said, putting an arm on my shoulder. "Just don't let her try to take over. Remember, you're number one, first choice."

"I'm kind of scared, Mindy. I don't even know what to do!"

"Ask Angel. She was captain and now you are.

I'm going to rush home and call Gary. What a relief!"

Relief? I didn't get it. But I was somewhat in shock at having been elected captain. Liz finally came over and congratulated me and said she hoped I didn't break a hip or anything so she'd have to take over. I made a mental note to watch my step around Liz.

Although the girls begged to be allowed to take stuff home, Miss Curry refused until it was paid for. "I'm responsible. Sorry," she said.

She gave each girl a cost sheet, and when she got to me she said she'd like to set up a conference some day soon. She didn't look too thrilled at having a newcomer elected captain.

I was not only not thrilled but seriously alarmed when I looked at the bill and saw the total amount. It was like the national debt. I hated to think of Mom's reaction. She was always dead set against spending money for what she called frivolous items. I'd have to convince her that Pom Pon equipment rated as one of life's necessities. It did, to me. After all, I was captain. How many other girls at Harrison Junior High could make that statement?

ELEVEN

WHEN MOM GOT HOME I FOLLOWED HER UP TO her room. While she was changing clothes, I did a replay of the election, leading up to the counting of the ballots.

"And you won," Mom said, slipping into her robe.

My mouth dropped open. "How did you know?"

She laughed. "Look at your face in the mirror."

I glanced above her dresser and saw bright spots of color on my cheeks.

"Mom," I said, jumping up and throwing my arms around her, "it's one of the biggest things that has ever happened to me."

"I'm glad," she said, hugging me.

"It's going to cost a lot," I said, into her shoulder.

"Oh?" She pulled away a little. "What is a *lot?*"

I told her.

"Oh, Clara! Just for . . ."

"It's important to me, Mom! Really important! I'll draw my own money out of the bank to pay for it."

"Clara! That's for your future."

"My future has to start some time." Tears came to my eyes. "I want it to be now. This year is important to me," I repeated.

Mom looked a little disappointed, I thought, but she managed to smile just a shade. "All right, go ahead, if that's what you want."

"Oh, Mom!" I almost squeezed the breath out of her. "I'll work next summer and make it all up after my big year is over!"

I spent almost two solid hours talking on the phone that evening as one member of the squad after another called to congratulate me and talk about the upcoming dance.

"If being elected captain means no other calls can get through in this house, you'd better resign," Mom said. "This is incredible."

"The girls are just excited," I said. "They'll simmer down."

"It's all so boring," Halcyon said. "Listening to the same thing over and over."

I was about to tell her she was free to leave when the phone rang again. Halcyon made a lunge for it. "For you," she said, handing me the receiver. "It's Jay Frank."

"Hi," I said. "What do you want? I can't talk."

I heard Halcyon give a snort as she left.

"Clara!" His voice trembled. "I've just gotta tell you this. Little Clara is eating out of my hand."

"What? Who?"

"I've been putting out bread, and now she takes it right from my hand."

"Jay Frank, what are you raving about?"

"My raccoon. Oh, I guess I forgot to tell you. You

84

said Racky was a dumb name, so I named her after you."

That would teach me to keep my mouth shut. "I'm really honored, Jay Frank," I said.

"That's okay. Want to come over? Maybe my friend will come back."

There was something a little heart-tugging about the way he said *my friend.* "Jay Frank, I'd like to one of these nights, but I've got to get going right now. I'll see you, though, okay?"

"Okay." He sounded wistful, but also resigned. Well . . . he had to learn sometime to stop leaning on me.

Mom was at her desk in the living room. "I'm off the phone," I told her, as I started upstairs. The front doorbell rang. I got it.

I also got the shock of my young life. It was Skip. Skip Svoboda. He wouldn't come in because a couple of the guys were out on the sidewalk waiting for him.

"Just heard you made captain," he said, with a slow, sweet smile, and his look just resting on my face. "Thought I'd stop by to see how you were taking it."

"In stride." The words came out by themselves.

"That's my girl." He glanced around at the guys who were making with the whistles. "I've gotta leave. See you."

"Sure." It's lucky I was leaning against the door jamb because my legs had gone limp.

I was sort of hoisting myself up the stairs when Mom called me back. "Who was that, and what was it all about?"

"That was Skip. You know. The guy I told you about."

"The one who used to like Angel?"

"Yeh, that's right."

"And what do you have to do with him?"

"Well . . . I guess he likes me, now."

"He . . . what?" Mom had on her principal-type expression.

I decided to try for the light approach even though the situation wasn't ideal for it. "Don't you think I'm likable?" I smiled and tried to look winning.

Mom didn't react. "Does being head of Pom Pon have anything to do with this sudden switch of *liking?*"

"It's not *sudden!*"

"Answer the question, Clara."

"The Pom Pon girls and the team do sort of hang around together, but no one can make anyone like anyone else. It's not a school code or anything like that."

"It just happens?"

"Sometimes." I felt hurt, I really did. "Mom, you want to know something? You don't give me any credit. Some people like me for who I am."

"That's the point. Who you are is different from what you are. I hope you don't confuse the two."

"Mom, you know what? You're making a big deal over nothing."

"All right. Just don't sell yourself short, Clara."

I said good-night, went upstairs to my room, and closed the door. Why did Mom have to get heavy just when everything was going my way? I guess she just wasn't ready to handle the fact that I had my own ideas. I wasn't like Laurel.

Skip liked me. Really liked me. I guess I could tell, from the way his eyes just practically caressed me. Caressed . . . what a beautiful word! Clara . . . caressed. Clara . . . the caressable.

And then, what he'd said at the last. *That's my girl.* Was I? Could I be? It seemed too good, too sudden to be true.

But it *was* true. Skip *had* meant it. He started hanging around me the very next day at school.

November came, and with it the first snow and frigid air. The Pom Pon girls, out in half-time on the football field, were solid goose bumps from ankle socks to undershorts. I knew it was cold, I could see it on my legs as we got back to the bleachers, but excitement kept me warm. Plus the thought, I'm Skip's girl. I still couldn't fully realize this had happened, even though everyone else took it for granted by now that Skip and I were a twosome.

It had come about so suddenly, without any kind of effort on my part. I didn't let myself question that, but still I couldn't help wondering at times how Angel felt about it. One day I finally broke down and asked her. I knew, being the type of person she is, that she'd level with me.

"Clara, I thought I'd told you," she said. "Skip and I have no interest in each other any more. The field is clear."

"How could you let go of him like that?" I persisted. "He's Number One. A personality."

Angel's eyelids flickered. "Maybe that's it. He used to be a *person*."

"You think there's something wrong with that?"

"Of course not, Clara. I've just lost interest, that's all."

I believed her. But then I had to switch to the other side of it. Had Skip lost interest in Angel, or was he just saving face?

One day after school when there was no practice,

Skip and I were sitting at a booth in the neighborhood junk food shop, which for a change was nearly empty. He was going on about all the games our team had lost, and how it didn't mean much.

"No one takes football seriously in junior high," he said, jiggling the ice in his glass. "Except maybe a few who aim for the high school varsity. Not me. I don't want to get mangled."

"I can see why," I said. I meant, *you're so good-looking*. I hoped he didn't think I meant he was cowardly. My mind was really on Skip and Angel and the way they'd liked each other last year, but I said, "Basketball's starting soon now, anyway."

"Yeh, and that's really my game. We're lining up practice now, did I tell you?"

"Yes, you did. I mean, I know. I mean . . ."

"I mean, I mean," he teased. "What do you mean?"

I almost fell apart when he smiled down at me that way, with that lazy, affectionate look in his eyes. "I guess I don't express myself very well," I mumbled. Something inside of me said, *just let it go at that, stop what you're about to say,* but I went on anyway. "I'm not like Angel."

"No, you're not," he said. "And that's in your favor."

I wanted to know why, but couldn't ask.

Skip shifted a little. "Angel's an all right kid, but it's kind of nice to be around someone whose looks are a contrast. Angel and I were too much of a matched pair."

"Oh? I think she's prettier than you." I was teasing, but Skip didn't get it.

"Angel's not all that good-looking," he said.

"Good looking! She's perfect!"

"She just lets on that she is." Skip ran a hand over his own blond hair, shifted again, and then put an arm around my shoulder. "You're the one who's perfect," he said.

He meant it. I just had to believe he meant it.

"Yeh," he said, "you and I are going to look good together at the dance."

I gripped my glass. "Dance?"

Skip laughed. "Come on, you know about it. Two weeks from Friday. Start thinking about what you're going to wear." He laughed again. "Besides that cute look."

Some kids came by then and joined us, and that was that.

I couldn't remember afterward what anyone had said.

TWELVE

WHEN I GOT HOME I SAW THAT THE LOCAL paper, lying on our kitchen table, was folded to *School News*. The Honor Roll list was circled. My name appeared on the A list and so did Halcyon's. I was a little surprised that my grades had averaged so high, since I hadn't put in too much effort. Halcyon, on the other hand, hit the books every night.

I shoved the paper aside. I didn't want to think about Halcyon. I didn't even want to think about grades. All I wanted to think about was Skip. And what he'd said. And about the dance. It would be our first real date! I'd have to think about what to wear, and cute looks weren't enough. Even Skip had said so. But I guess he was kidding. Even so, I wasn't about to take any chances.

My mind was somewhat muddled during dinner. While Halcyon was rattling on about making the Honor Roll and how it didn't really mean much because this school was so below what she was used to

I thought, *you fake. You want and work for approval. Except where I'm concerned.* What grudge did Halcyon have against me? And why?

Then my thoughts would switch to Skip and how we were going to the dance together. But how was I going to break the news to Mom? I didn't think she'd be too crazy about the idea. Although I mentioned Skip's name from time to time and got calls from him, I'd never let on that I was his *girl.* Mom wouldn't tune in to that type of thinking. Her life was K-6 where kids were kids. I doubted she realized what a different game it was in junior high. If only Laurel had fallen in love at my age, things would be easier for me now.

"How's Laurel?" I asked, as long as my mind was on her. "What did she have to say in her letter today?"

"Nothing much." Mom leaned her elbows on the table, cupped one hand on the other, and looked at me, smiling. "She didn't need to write much. Because we're going to see her."

"Great! When's she coming home?"

"She's not." Mom smiled even more. "We're going there."

"Really? To New York?"

"That's where she lives now," Halcyon said.

"When are we going?" I asked.

"During Thanksgiving vacation. My friend Annie is taking care of hotel reservations."

I glanced at Halcyon, relieved that we weren't lined up to stay at her apartment. She had a grumpy look on her face. "Annie's my aunt," she said. "My great-aunt."

So what? Who was making any claims? "I don't know her very well," I said.

"And she really doesn't know you." From the look Halcyon gave me, you'd think I'd pulled a fast one.

"It works out fine," Mom went on, still wrapped in her happy thoughts. "We can all fly out together and back, and yet have our own little separate visits. I wonder if Annie has changed."

"She looks good, considering her age," Halcyon said. "Very elegant."

"Oh, dear. I'd better get something to wear before we go out." Mom's glance fell on me. "And you, too, Clara. A coat, especially. That ski jacket is not appropriate."

"That's for sure," Halcyon said.

"I need other clothes, too," I told Mom. "For school parties. And of course, New York."

"You ought to wait and then hit the shops as soon as you get there," Halcyon said. "My mother can steer you to the best places."

I ignored her. "Let's not wait," I said to Mom. "As you say yourself, if something has to be done, do it."

"We'll see." Mom got up. "Whose turn is it to do the dishes?"

"Mine," I said.

I really didn't mind doing the dishes any more because Skip usually called around this time, and I hated it when Halcyon picked up the phone.

They had no sooner left than it rang. "Hello," I said, using my soft voice.

"Clara? This is Sheri. Is Jay Frank there?"

"Jay Frank? No, I haven't seen him."

"That kid! Then why doesn't he answer the

phone? I'm going to be stuck here at the office for another hour, and I'm worried."

"I'll go check on him for you. And call you back."

"Thanks, sweetie."

I tossed on a cardigan of Mom's that was hanging by the back doorway and then noticed the lights were on in the basement. "Jay Frank, are you down there?" I called.

"Yes."

"What's the idea, hanging around at this hour," I yelled as he came upstairs. "Your mom's worried sick. Why didn't you call her or let us know you were down there in the cellar?"

"I guess I forgot. After Angel and Fergy left, I just kept on holding and petting those little rats. They're all friends with me now."

"Yeh, tell me about it. But first call your mom and say you're okay. Then I'll take you home."

"Will you stay for a while?" he asked, as we started out a few minutes later. "You keep promising to come over, but you never do."

"I have homework every night, remember." I felt a little guilty, even though my social life and all was none of Jay Frank's business. "You ought to leave on a light when you take off." He was fumbling for the lock. "It gets dark early now. In fact, you ought not to leave, period, when your mother's not home." I sounded like quite the little mother myself, but it was habit.

I threw on a few lights, including the one on the patio.

Jay Frank's dishes, from whatever he had eaten after school, were neatly lined up in the drain rack.

93

"Want some ice cream?" he asked. "We have some thawed raspberries I could put on the top."

"Sure, sounds good. Go light on the ice cream, though. I'm watching my weight." I let him dish it up because it made him feel big. Meanwhile I strolled over to the window by the patio. "What's that stuff out there on the paper plate?"

"I put out food for my night friends."

"Oh. Little Clara and that crowd?"

"Yeh." Jay Frank was digging away at the ice cream container. "Is this enough?"

I turned to check. "Fine." I got a drink of water, then walked back to the window. And then I yelled.

"What's the matter, Clara?" There was panic in Jay Frank's voice.

There was more panic in mine. "That . . . that rat! That giant rat!" I leaped to a chair. "Out there, eating the food!"

Jay Frank crept to the window and looked out. Then he turned to me. "You dummy! That's just an opossum."

"Opossum? Are you sure? It looks like a rat to me!"

"That's just because of his tail. Opossums have very long tails. They can wrap them around things."

I folded my hands under my arms, quick. "Why didn't you tell me you had repulsive animals like that coming around here?"

"I had the feeling you might not come over if you knew."

"You had the right feeling."

"But he's cute, Clara. Come over here and take a close look at those little feet. The back ones have thumbs, just like ours, almost."

"Speak for yourself." I was off the chair by now, but keeping my distance from the window. "Come back and eat your ice cream. It's melting."

Jay Frank sat down and dug in, and I sat opposite. The dinner guest outside had somewhat affected my appetite, but still, raspberries were raspberries, especially in November.

"Did you know opossums travel alone?" Jay Frank asked.

"That doesn't surprise me. If I were one, it's for sure I wouldn't want to look at someone else as ugly as I was."

"Do you know opossums are marsupials?" Jay Frank asked. "That means they carry their babies around in a pouch."

"Could we maybe change the subject? I could read all this in a book, if I was interested."

"That's what I did. Let me tell you just one more thing, Clara. This is really interesting. When opossum babies are born, they're really tiny. I mean, *really*. They're so tiny that twenty of them could fit right into that teaspoon of yours."

Raspberries flew into the air, followed by my teaspoon, followed by me. I ran to the sink and gagged.

"Are you sick, Clara?" Jay Frank sounded really upset.

"No." I pulled myself together. It was just a little retch, nothing more.

"I'm sorry. I keep forgetting how you don't like little animals, but if you'd just . . ."

He looked so guilty and so pleading, I wanted to reach out to hug him, but instead, I stooped to pick up the spoon. Jay Frank bent down at the same time and our heads bumped.

"Oh, sorry." I leaned forward and kissed him lightly on the forehead where we'd bumped.

"Don't do that!" He shrank away.

"Don't do that? A little kiss? How come?"

"I don't like it. Besides . . ."

"Besides what?"

"I don't want to be . . . headed for trouble."

I stared at him. "What are you babbling about? What do you mean, headed for trouble?"

"Halcyon said *you* are. She said, 'I know what she's *really* like.'" His look was somewhat accusing. "Well, you do have a boyfriend, don't you?"

"So what! It's none of her business. That low-life creep!"

Jay Frank jumped up. "Don't call Halcyon a creep! She's my friend!"

"Oh, you and your friends! Anyone . . . or anything that pays the least bit of attention to you is your *friend*. Sometimes I wonder about you. I really do."

"Everyone needs friends!"

"Yeh, well, if you're going to palsy up to raccoons and opossums and rats, not to mention that weasel Halcyon, you can just cross *me* off your list!"

I didn't mean it, not seriously, but Jay Frank looked me straight in the eye and said, "I guess I don't like you any more, anyway."

"It's mutual." I snatched up the sweater and headed toward the door, expecting to hear a pleading, *Clara . . . I didn't mean it,* but Jay Frank didn't utter a word.

I went home and upstairs. I wanted to pound on Halcyon's door and ask her if Skip had called, but

I didn't want to give her the satisfaction in case he hadn't.

Headed for trouble. What a stupid thing to say to a little kid. I knew from experience that Halcyon said anything that popped into her mind, but she ought to learn a little control.

For that matter, I shouldn't have shot off my mouth that way to Jay Frank. But I'd make it up to him.

For now, I thought, as I closed the door to my bedroom behind me, I was just going to concentrate on Skip and what he had said to me in the booth. *You're the one who's perfect. You and I are going to look great together at the dance.*

Two weeks from now! The dance! I'd circle it on my calendar and each day have a count-down.

I found a red pen, found the Friday, and drew a heart around it. And then my fingers stiffened. That was the Friday after Thanksgiving! *The* Friday. The Friday we'd be in New York City!

I threw myself on the bed and banged my feet in frustration. What could I do? I couldn't get Mom . . . no, there was no way I could get Mom to stay home or let me stay home. I had to go. And Skip would be . . . what? Furious? Hurt? He might be so furious and hurt he'd ask someone else. I was so shook up I couldn't even cry. I just began rolling back and forth in misery.

Finally I got up and got ready for bed, but all I could think about later, as I kicked and tossed, was how my life was about to be ruined, and at such an early age. I knew, if I fell asleep, which was doubtful, that all I'd dream about was Skip, going to the dance with somebody else.

But strangely enough, the next morning, the only dream I remembered was one about Jay Frank. He was lost, and I could hear him crying. But I couldn't find him.

THIRTEEN

"DON'T WORRY ABOUT IT," SKIP SAID, WHEN I finally got around to telling him. This was two—I repeat two—days before vacation.

"Relax," he said, and he gave a little laugh at what must have been a really blank look on my face. "No sweat."

Of all the reactions I'd expected from Skip, including anger, revenge, disgust (at my waiting so long to tell), this was the one I hadn't even considered. "You're not mad?" I just couldn't believe it.

"Cutie, these things happen. Just have yourself a real good time in New York. And don't do anything I wouldn't do."

I stood, weak with relief, watching Skip shove things into his locker. Gary and Mindy came along.

"Hey, too bad about you guys and the dance," Gary said, as they came close. And then, over his shoulder as they kept walking, he added, "Shake 'em up in Milwaukee."

"What?" I stared after them and then looked

down at Skip's back, as he knelt to get something from the bottom of his locker. "What makes them think I'm going to Milwaukee?"

Skip shuffled shoes and notebooks around for several seconds, and when he finally stood up, he didn't quite look me in the eye. "As a matter of fact, my folks are going up to visit relatives and they raised a big stink about my having to go along. So kid, I won't be around, either."

"Oh!" It was like lights coming on after a crime movie and you know you're safe. "Then it works out perfectly. We'll be away together!"

It sounded funny, but we both knew what I meant.

"You're cute, Clara," Skip said with that look that made me weak. "I'll miss you. But it's a load off my mind."

He'd been afraid to tell me, too!

Had Skip thought I'd get hysterical . . . maybe go off to the dance with someone else? How wonderful! Whoever would have dreamed that our being separated during vacation would really bring us closer together like this?

The eight o'clock flight was the earliest we could get on Wednesday night and even so, the plane was jammed. Everyone, though, was in a cheerful holiday mood, except possibly me. I couldn't help wishing that everything had worked out differently and I was going to the dance, with Skip.

I snuggled against my new camel coat and then fumbled around for the seat belt. I flipped Halcyon's furred cuff out of the way. She flipped it right back. "Do you *mind?*" she said. "These window seats are narrow, you know that."

100

She was the one who'd made a rush for it. "And ry to keep your feet off my rat photos. I don't want hem all mooshed up."

I pushed them as far away as I could. "Why'd you aave to bring them along, anyway?"

"Why? Because my parents are very interested in ny talent. Especially my father."

The word *father* suddenly made me feel forlorn. I stared straight ahead. I could feel Halcyon's eyes on me.

Finally she heaved an impatient sigh. "I hope you're not going to be this way all weekend. It's not forever, you know. You'll soon be back in his arms."

"Wh-what?" Really, I was confused.

"Everyone knows what's going on with you two. Except maybe your mother." We both glanced at Mom, who seemed to be dozing. "But if you don't mind, I'd just as soon my parents didn't know. I'm certainly not going to tell them."

"Are you talking about . . . *Skip?*"

Halcyon rolled her eyes upward. "As though you didn't know!"

I was so angry I reached forward and grabbed the first thing I could find from the magazine packet. It was a throw-up bag. I shoved it back and took the flyer of all the things you could buy from the airline.

"There's nothing *going on*," I muttered, catching only blurs of merchandise as I turned the pages. "You know, Halcyon, you have a perverted mind." Before she could recover, I added, "And I don't appreciate the little remarks you made to Jay Frank, either. He's just a kid, and you should take that into consideration before you sound off."

Halcyon adjusted her headband, pulled her hair back from her neck, and looked out the window.

The male flight attendant came along with the liquor cart and asked if we wanted cokes or 7-up. We both said, "Cokes," and Halcyon added, "with a twist of lemon."

He gave her a look and handed her a plain coke.

When they brought around the dinner trays, Mom perked up and so did Halcyon. I tried to eat but couldn't get it down.

"If you're not going to touch your dessert, I'll have it," Halcyon said. As we exchanged her empty container for my full one, I marveled at how mere food could bring her around. But maybe she was just easing into a better attitude before we met her parents.

To my dismay, Mr. and Mrs. Hart weren't at the airport to collect Halcyon. Mom explained why. "We arranged for them to pick up Halcyon at our hotel," she said. "No use for them to battle the traffic all the way out here."

If they had, they could have given us a ride, but we finally got a cab and in due time arrived at the hotel. A youngish couple rushed toward us in the lobby and hugged Halcyon as best they could around all the stuff she was carrying.

Halcyon put on the grand performance, saying how great it was to be back in civilization and how she felt like leaning over and kissing the ground. We were standing on a maroon-colored carpet at the time.

Her father had curly hair and a mustache and was a little bit on the heavy side. As he talked with Mom, he had an arm draped around Halcyon's shoulder. They looked a lot alike.

Mrs. Hart was tiny and stylish in her fur coat and sleek boots. I thought the dark glasses were a bit much at this time of night, and I also couldn't see why such a simple hairdo—free swinging from a center part—called for the services of a top stylist, as Halcyon often saw fit to mention.

While I was sizing her up, Mrs. Hart turned and said, "Clara, you're every bit as pretty as Halcyon said you were. I wish you could get her to wear a touch of makeup." She studied Halcyon. "But of course, the first priority is weight." She sighed.

Mr. Hart came forward, shook hands, thanked Mom again, and said they should get going. Halcyon hesitated and looked as though she were going to hug Mom, but then she too, shook hands. "See you," she said to me.

I wondered, as I watched them walk away, why she had mentioned my looks to her mother. When Halcyon talked to me, it was always her mother's looks that were so outstanding. I guess I never would understand that girl.

Mom, the bellhop, and I got into the elevator along with some kid of about eight who had stringy blond hair, blue rimmed glasses, and several candy bars in her fist. She leaned toward the buttons, huffed out a breath, and number seven lit up. After she got off, the bellboy told me it's heat, not pressure, that activates the buttons. I wished Fergy and I could be in an elevator some time. I'd like to dazzle him with that inside information. Fergy . . . Angel. They seemed so far away. They *were* far away. I'd rather be there, even in the rat cellar, than here.

"When is Laurel coming over?" I asked Mom, when we were alone in the room. There were two double beds.

"Later. Why don't you take your bath and then get into bed and watch TV?"

"Could I go down and get a candy bar first? I'm starved."

She gave me money and the room key. Going down, there were others in the elevator, but coming back up I had it all to myself. I huffed out my breath on number 9 and sure enough, it lit up.

My spirits lit up, too. You know how that happens sometimes. You're feeling depressed and blah, and then all of a sudden, like a switch being flicked, you see things in a different light. Right now the low feelings that came from being away from Skip and on the plane with Halcyon left me. I began thinking it wasn't bad, being in a hotel and having a holiday in a big city and, of course, seeing my sister after all these weeks.

My plan was to lie in bed, awake, until she got there, but I must have drifted off. I felt Mom lift the pillows from behind my head and shift me down in the bed, and then later I was vaguely aware of voices, and lips brushing my forehead, and another body in the bed.

The next morning when I woke up, Laurel was still asleep, her lovely, slim fingers pressed together as though in prayer, under her cheek. I propped my head on my hand and looked at her.

"Let her sleep," Mom whispered, passing by the bed, but at that instant, Laurel jerked upright and her hand reached to the bedside table for a clock, I guess, that wasn't there.

"Laurel." Mom gave a nervous laugh. "You're with us. No practice today."

My sister slumped with relief, then fully woke up. "Mother!"

Mom sat on the edge of the bed and held Laurel close. "Do you always wake up in such a panic?" She smoothed the long brown hair.

"Always. I'm always afraid I'll be late." Laurel had her arms around Mom, too, and she snuggled her face against Mom's neck. "Oh, it's so good to have you here and to have . . . to have a holiday." She stayed that way for a moment, but then it was like click, click, back to business. She pulled away. "But of course, I love Juilliard. It's a struggle, but worth every minute of it."

"I'm glad," Mom said. Her hands moved to Laurel's arms. "You're thinner than ever."

"You're plain skinny," I said.

Laurel whipped around and with a half-tackle flattened me against the pillow. "Baby Bunting!" she squealed. She kissed me and tickled me the way she used to when I was real little.

I tickled her back, and we were all over the bed, grabbing at pillows for protection. "Don't call me 'Baby Bunting,'" I said, giving her a jab in the ribs. She really was skinny.

"He's gone to get a rabbitskin, to wrap the Baby Bunting in!" she said, laughing and dodging the pillow.

"You know I always hated that song," I said. "Wrapped in rabbitskin. Ick."

"Some day, baby, I'll wrap you in mink," she said, slipping away from me and out of the bed. "Some day when I'm rich and famous."

She stood for a moment in her nightgown, hair tangled over her shoulders. She was quiet now. "I was just talking," she said after a moment, glancing at Mother. "I don't need to be rich or famous. I just need to be good."

I lay back with a pillow cradled to my chest. I hated to think what would happen to my sister if she wasn't good. Good enough, in her opinion. What happened to pianists who didn't quite make it?

To my surprise, after that big bit from Halcyon about *my Aunt Annie,* Mom's friend Annie Schuyler was set to have Thanksgiving dinner with us late Thursday afternoon.

"How come?" I asked Mom. "Why won't she be going with the relatives?"

"She sees Kate and Jeff—Halcyon's parents—often enough. She wants to see *me.* Us. We used to be so close át college."

Boy, that was a million centuries ago. "So Halcyon will be with just her folks, then?"

"Clara, I know this is vacation, but would you still do me the favor of not starting sentences with the word *so?* As for Halcyon, she's going with her parents to the home of friends in Long Island. Isn't that right, Laurel?"

"Somewhere like that. Mother, is this going to be a fancy restaurant? I forgot to bring heels."

"You're fine." Mom's look rested on the dress Laurel was wearing. "But is that it? Your best? It's . . ."

"Out-of-date," I said.

"I just don't have time to go shopping. I have the money you sent, Mother. But I don't have the . . ."

"We'll go tomorrow," Mom said. "Laurel, you've got to get some clothes, with recitals coming up and . . ."

"Clothes don't count."

"Even so." Mom's mind was made up. She excused herself to take a shower.

"Laurel," I said, when I heard the water running, "why don't you get what's-her-name—Kate—to take you shopping? She's very *now*." Slight imitation of Halcyon.

"No, if I have to shop, I'd rather it be with Mother. She has good taste, and it's more to my style."

"What do you think of her . . . Kate? Is she stuck up?"

"You ought to call her Mrs. Hart."

"Oh, I will. But *is* she?"

Laurel bit one of her nails. "Not stuck up. But kind of snappish. With other people. Her husband. But not me. She treats me with a sort of . . ." Laurel gave a tiny, embarrassed laugh. "Awe. You know, as though I weren't quite real."

Laurel did have that effect on people. I guess it was her delicate look. And her talent. Plus, she was so gentle.

"Mr. Hart is more natural," she said. "I don't see a lot of them. They're tied up with the gallery, and they go out most evenings. I have the run of the place when I'm there. It's perfect."

She must have seen something on my face, because almost guiltily, she asked, "How is it for you? With Halcyon?"

"Oh, okay." Mom came out just then, and we got ready to go.

Annie Schuyler gave Mom a grand welcoming embrace, and me a big hug, and a smaller one for Laurel, whom she saw now and then. All the while the maitre d' was making nervous gestures toward the waiting table; the restaurant was packed.

"It's so grand to be with my favorite people," Annie said. "This calls for a drink." She ordered something on the rocks and Mom took the same. Laurel passed altogether, but I ordered a coke. "With lemon." I got it!

Aunt Annie (mentally I kept calling her that, although outwardly I avoided calling her anything) was older looking than I remembered. Or maybe it was just the stress and strain of city life showing up. Her skin wasn't as smooth as Mom's, but she wore makeup—not too much—to cover. Her hair was waved and a kind of ash-blond, probably tinted. The only woman I saw in all of New York City with gray hair, besides Mom, was a washroom attendant.

Annie and Mom tried to keep the conversation general during the meal, but it kept circling back to college days. I didn't mind. It was great, just being in that fancy place and being able to order anything. "Anything, darling, anything you like," Annie kept insisting. And it was interesting to see Mom from a different view. The drink may have helped, and then the dinner wine, but I think it was mostly the talk that made her seem younger, and more carefree. Even her laugh was lighter.

Laurel must have noticed it too, because she'd look at Mom, then look down, and smile.

"Do you remember me, dear?" Annie suddenly said, leaning toward me. "From the last time I visited you?"

"I remember the cat statue you brought."

"Clara!" Mom's rebuke drifted into a laugh. "Really . . ."

"She's adorable," Annie said. "I've got myself an

adorable godchild." Lucky she was looking at Mom when she said that because it's for sure I'd forgotten about the godmother thing. She took my hand across the table. There was a knockout pearl and diamond ring on her little finger. "Could I borrow this child tomorrow?" she asked Mom. "I want to know her. You and Laurel will be busy shopping anyway."

"Well, if Clara . . ."

"Then it's all settled!" Annie said. "We'll have such fun. And I'll tell her all your girlhood secrets, Jessie."

Mom laughed. "Oh, not all. Please, Annie, not all."

As it turned out, the secret told was on Halcyon. But in a way, it was more a plain truth. An answer.

I thought it would be strange, spending most of the day with a woman I hardly knew. Person-to-person, I mean. But Annie Schuyler started talking as though we were continuing a conversation from last week, and I didn't feel uneasy at all.

Her apartment wasn't big, but it had a feeling of comfort, with its flowery, soft-cushioned furniture and a sort of gardeny look.

"Did you do this all yourself?" I asked, and then blushed. She was a decorator, after all. "I love it."

"Take a look at the bedroom. It's in Far East. And I did it before China became the thing."

I liked the lacquered chests, and screen, and oriental rug, but it wasn't a room I'd like to sleep in.

"The kitchen's not much," Annie said. "Cooking's not one of my talents, so that's why we're going out to lunch."

She took me to a place where, like yesterday, the

109

waiters seemed to know her. I guessed she was rich, or at least well off.

"Tell me," she said, after we'd ordered, "does that darling baby still live next to you?"

"Baby? There's no ba . . . oh! You mean Jay Frank?"

"That's the one. Such a pet!"

"Yeah. He gets on my nerves sometimes, but . . ."

"He's like your little brother and you forgive him."

"I guess that's right. We had a run-in about rats not long ago, but we made it up."

"*Rats?* Real rats?"

I told her about the experiments and Angel and Fergy, and then I got around to how Halcyon was photographing the whole schmeer. I tried to make a joke of it, but it fell kind of flat.

"So she's still on that camera kick," Aunt Annie said, disgust showing in her tone. "I've never before known a child with such a one-track mind."

I felt a little defensive toward Halcyon. "She's good at photography, though. And some people have just one interest in life. Like Laurel."

"But music, my dear. That's different."

The waiter who brought our food kept hovering around until Aunt Annie waved him away. "You were saying?" she said, turning back to me.

Instead of going on with the one-track mind topic, I switched to what I really wanted to discuss. "Could I ask you something? Confidentially?"

"Absolutely."

"Why did Halcyon actually come out to live with us?" I touched the napkin to my lips. "I've heard first one story, and then another."

Aunt Annie moved the anchovies to one side of her salad. "I assumed you knew. Kate and Jeff couldn't swing the tuition at boarding school this year, and they wouldn't let me handle it. And that stubborn girl refused—*refused*—to come down off her high horse and go to public school. So finally, to save the peace, and for another reason, I suggested they send her out to you."

I hesitated, then blurted out, "And what was the other reason?" Had Halcyon really gotten into trouble because of the school pranks? I'd never believed that. She wasn't the type.

"The other reason," Aunt Annie said, "was that I hoped your mother could take that girl and instill some common sense into her. Jessie's so levelheaded, and she's done a marvelous job raising you two girls."

I didn't know what to say to that, so I just started eating my salad.

"Of course," Aunt Annie continued, "I haven't seen a lot of you, darling, but I remembered you as such a nice, outgoing girl and I trusted you still were. And you are." She patted my hand.

I forked the lettuce around my plate. "You didn't tell Halcyon that, did you?"

"But of course I did. We had a little chat before she left, and I expressly mentioned she could pick up a few pointers from you."

I felt sick. If Aunt Annie had done a study of the best way to do me in, she couldn't have come up with a better weapon. There isn't a kid alive who likes being compared unfavorably to another. But some grown-ups, especially those who aren't around young people, think it's the sure-fire way to shape up a kid who misses the mark. I could understand that, but it had certainly shot any hope of a decent relationship between Halcyon and me.

111

"She is getting along, isn't she?" Aunt Annie was almost begging for a pat on the head.

Well, it was done. "Halcyon's doing great in school," I said. And then I quickly changed the subject to Pom Pon.

Aunt Annie tried to be interested, she really did. But after a while, when I was describing our routines and how we were working up to the big playoffs in January, I caught her sneaking a look at her watch.

"I guess," I said with an apologetic little laugh, "I get carried away on the subject of Pom Pon."

"Not at all," she said, trying to make it sound genuine. "Young people have to live in the present. The future's too scary."

"I don't think about the future."

She took my hand. "Neither did I, at your age. But before you know it, it's tomorrow, and the year beyond."

I didn't like that kind of talk. I didn't want to think about years beyond. I wanted things to stay this way forever . . . being captain of the Pom Pon squad and being Skip's girl. That's what was important. The tomorrows didn't matter.

Annie took me sightseeing in the afternoon. The next day—Saturday—Mom, Laurel, and I did a lot of things and before I knew it, Sunday had come and we were all back at La Guardia Airport.

FOURTEEN

Since, in my put-off way, I'd never got around to buying postcards, at the airport I got Jay Frank a little souvenir Statue of Liberty.

"I hate copies of things like that," Halcyon said. "They took too tacky."

"I can't afford the original," I said.

Halcyon walked away, then, to the candy bar section, and I quickly bought a comb shaped like a fish for Skip. It wasn't much, just something to show I'd been thinking of him.

Halcyon's parents were guarding our hand luggage in the waiting area of the airport. I guess they'd convinced Halcyon to leave some stuff at home, since she'd be coming back for Christmas. When they made the boarding announcement, Halcyon's father held out the famous envelope of rat photos. "Here, don't forget this," he said.

"Those are for you!" Halcyon said. "For the gallery!"

He laughed. "Oh, come on. So far we don't show

photographs and even if we did . . ." the way he
sort of thrust them toward Halcyon showed what he
thought of them.

She snatched them, and her look was a mixture of
fury, disappointment, and, I think, a little embar-
rassment. I turned away but heard her say, "You
told me!"

"I told you that maybe . . . maybe some day
when you're older and professional enough . . ."

"Yeh, sure, *some day!* What about now?"

"Young lady," Mrs. Hart said, "we're all getting
a bit bored with this fixation of yours about cam-
eras. Can't you just be a *child,* doing normal things
like . . ." Her voice drifted off. *Like Clara,* she had
been about to say. I knew it.

People must have moved between us then, because I heard a blur of other voices, and finally Mom
came back from the newsstand where she'd bought a
magazine. We waited at the corridor, she shook
hands with Halcyon's parents, and the three of us
went on into the plane.

Halcyon was very quiet. She had the look of a
dog that had been told to go away and not bother
anyone. Not that I thought her folks should have
said, "Oh, hey, these photos are great and we'll
show them in the gallery." I mean, you can't nau-
seate customers just to show off your kid's work.
But her father could have shown a little more approval. Approval. That's what Halcyon wanted, all
right, but she came on so strong, she even put off her
own parents.

"You're taking back the photos?" Mom asked, as
Halcyon jammed them into the overhead. "I
thought . . ."

"She needs them for the science fair," I broke in.

I don't know how I happened to come up with that. "They go along with Angel and Fergy's experiment. Isn't that right, Halcyon?"

"Yeah." If she had any feeling about my helping her out, she wasn't going to show it.

"This is really nice," Skip said, when I gave him the comb. "But you didn't need to bring me back anything. Except yourself."

"Did you miss me?" Why did I have to *say* it? I hated myself for letting me say it.

Skip just gave me the look. "Guess."

I still got a tingle when Skip talked like that. I saw him almost every day at practice, at lunch, and at my locker, like now; but I guess I'd never get used to the idea that I was his girl. "I had a good time in New York," I said.

"Yeh? Meet any guys?"

"Skip!" I gave him a playful punch. "We went sightseeing and to plays. We saw a super musical with lots of kids in the cast. It was based on . . ."

I turned to see who or what it was that had caught Skip's attention down the hall. Liz. Liz Halston. She passed out of our view.

"You were saying?" Skip asked, his eyes resting on me again.

"Oh, nothing." What did Skip care about some musical in another town? I had to learn how to keep his interest and hold it. "Tell me about Milwaukee." I said it with a little tease in my tone, the way I'd seen a girl do on a TV show.

"You don't want to hear about Milwaukee." He brushed my cheek with the back of his fingers. I think he might have kissed me, maybe, but just then a custodian rounded the corner pushing a big

115

trash can on wheels and that sort of killed the romantic mood.

I'd noticed in other years that the cold months seem to drag on forever, but December was never like that. This year, it was a whirlwind.

It seemed everyone was caught up in the holiday spirit and there were all kinds of school events crowding the calendar. Most of all, in my life, were the games and practice in between, plus two after-game parties at girls' houses. The parties, I have to say, weren't much in themselves because the parents kept checking to see that the lights were on. No one ever danced, and the stereos blasted so loud you couldn't carry on a conversation. But being close to Skip was all that I asked.

I was really on target with my POPULARITY MUSTS list, which I checked out every now and then. I felt (without trying to be conceited about it) that I was now one of the cutest girls in the school. Not a great beauty like some, but I played up everything I had. I was really in with the Pom Pon crowd and I had the number one boy at school wrapped around my finger. I was on the party list, and while my clothes wouldn't put me in the best-dressed category, I'd learned to switch separates around, and Angel and I traded clothes. My grades so far were keeping up there, and I went out of my way to be friendly to everyone, even teachers.

The next big challenge was to throw a slumber party for the Pom Pon girls at our house, and that I intended to do during the Christmas vacation. It was the perfect time. I'd try to get Laurel to go off somewhere with Mom early in the evening until the party got into gear. Of course, Halcyon would be with her family in New York. That was important. Even though Halcyon had toned down some lately, her kind of talk wouldn't go too well with the Pom Pon crowd.

So everything was going according to plan until late in December, when Mom gave me some really unsettling news.

"I talked with Laurel again," she said, coming into my room one evening. "Her cold isn't any better." Mom frowned. "I think she's more sick than she admits, because she's actually stayed home from classes, and you know your sister."

"She'll feel better once she gets home," I said, checking off a homework assignment.

"If. I'm not going to let her travel in a state of near pneumonia."

"Mom, she'd feel terrible not being with us at Christmas!"

"Then we'd simply go out there."

"We *can't!*" The thought of what the girls would say if I called off the party hit me like a rock. "We were just there a month ago!"

"So . . . we'll go again if necessary. The Thanksgiving trip was a form of vacation and to check out Laurel's situation. And of course, I enjoyed seeing Annie again. But this may be a necessity. I thought I ought to warn you before you made plans."

"I already have," I said, doing graffiti on a pad. "You know about the party."

Mom took a deep breath. "Well, we'll see. It's still a week off." She paused at the door. "You might send Laurel a note." Her look seemed to add, *since you're so concerned.*

The next day I sent Laurel a get-well card. It worked. By the end of the week we got the good news that Laurel was feeling better and would come home as planned. I was glad for her, of course, but I must say I mostly breathed a sigh of relief for myself.

Our plans worked out that we took Halcyon to the airport and picked up Laurel on the same trip.

Laurel looked paler and thinner than before, but she was all hepped up on the idea of coming home. I guess she missed us a lot. Halcyon's parents were so wrapped up in the gallery and social life they weren't much company.

Although Laurel seemed better during the next few days, I could hear her coughing from Halcyon's room at night and sometimes hear her get up and go downstairs. One night I crept down to see what she was doing. I found her wrapped in a blanket in a chair in the living room staring at the lighted Christmas tree.

"Is something wrong?" I asked.

"Oh, no. I just couldn't sleep." She opened the blanket. "Come, bunny, talk to me." I cuddled beside her.

"Want some hot chocolate?"

Laurel laughed. "No. What I need is something to ease my conscience."

"Are you kidding?"

"Here I am, taking it easy, when I should be catching up on work I missed when I was sick. That's silly, I guess. I should just let myself relax and make up for lost time later."

"That's right," I said. "I'm always reading about celebrities hiding out somewhere to recharge their batteries. Now don't laugh," I said, giving her a nudge. "You're going to be famous some day."

Laurel's arm stiffened a little. "Is that all you care about?"

"Well, aren't you going to be a concert pianist, playing in halls everywhere? Even Europe? Maybe Japan?"

"That's the highest rung, all right. But if I don't make it, I'm not going off the deep end."

"Laurel! You'd settle for less?"

"I'd settle for being the best of whatever I can possibly be."

"You can be whatever you want to be." I stared at the tree. "But, of course, it does help to know the right people." Without Angel, I was thinking, I'd never have made Pom Pon.

Laurel turned and looked at me. "Bunny! That's a warped attitude. I'm surprised at you."

"It's the way things work," I said. "Everywhere. You just don't know the ways of the world, Laurel."

We sat quietly for a few minutes, looking at the tree. It wasn't the showy type. It was full and fragrant and familiar, with toyland figures we'd had ever since I could remember. The lights were the old-time ones, too, not miniature, and they didn't flicker. It was very comforting sitting there with Laurel, being close, and not really needing to talk. After a while, though, I got kind of cramped and sleepy. "You ready to go back to bed?"

Laurel stirred, but then her arm around me tensed a little. "Clara?"

"Ummmm?"

"If I didn't really reach the top . . . would you be awfully disappointed? In me?"

"Oh, Laurel!" I leaned my head against her shoulder. "I'm sorry." My lips were against the lace at the neck of her nightgown. "It's you we love. Not what you might be."

She cupped her hand around the back of my head

and kissed my hair. "I'm glad. I knew. But it's good to hear."

"Shall we go back to bed?" I covered a yawn.

We went upstairs, and playing the little mother, I tucked Laurel in and kissed her good-night. "Sleep tight, and don't let the bedbugs bite," I said.

Later, lying awake, I got the strange thought, *In a way they're a little alike, Laurel and Halcyon. They both know where they want to go. Only Laurel's like a butterfly and Halcyon's like a bulldozer.*

Christmas was . . . what shall I say? Christmas like always. We had people over, including Jay Frank and Sheri and some of Mom's faculty friends. Jay Frank went bonkers over the toy car wash Halcyon and I had gone in on together (her idea), but for which she still hadn't paid her share (also her idea).

The day after, Angel came over to run her rat routine. By this time the little critters were onto the trick of racing down the runway, pressing the lever, and getting the goodies.

"Couldn't you just throw them a handful and let them goof off and enjoy the holidays?" I asked.

Angel looked shocked. "And ruin everything we've worked so hard to build up? Oh, Clara, you're kidding."

"Yeh. Hey . . ." I took hold of her hand. "Is that a new ring?"

"It's . . . yes. Halcyon gave it to me."

"*Halcyon?*" She'd given me knee socks. "Is it supposed to be a friendship ring? With that stone in it?"

Angel pulled away and, for once, looked embarrassed. "I didn't want to take it, but she insisted. She said good friends give good gifts. All I gave her was a nice barrette."

I tried to sound unconcerned. "Since when have you two become such good friends?"

Angel hesitated. "We're not really. I mean, I've tried to be friendly to her because she doesn't seem to have anyone. Except you, of course," she added, with a quick look.

"What happened to that crowd she ran with before?"

"I guess she had a falling out with one of the girls, especially. Halcyon's pretty outspoken."

"Don't I know!"

"So lately she's been hanging around Fergy and me quite a lot. She gave him a pocket calculator for Christmas, but he wouldn't accept it. I wish now I hadn't accepted this ring, but she said it was something of hers that she wanted me to have. I didn't want to hurt her feelings. It's kind of sad that . . ." Her voice drifted away.

Seeing Angel in that mood, it seemed almost as though our friendship had drifted a little, too. "You know what?" I said, leaning forward. "I think you should change your mind and come to the party Thursday night. You know everyone, and you'd fit right into the scene."

"Is the whole Pom Pon crowd going to be here?"

"Liz can't make it, and a couple of others, but most can. Come on, Angel."

"No, I don't think so." She twisted the ring absently and for a moment I thought she'd take it off, but she didn't. "It wouldn't be fair."

Fair? What did she mean? Because she was no longer on the squad? Or did she mean—could she possibly mean—that it wouldn't be fair for her to come when she knew I'd purposely planned the party for when Halcyon wouldn't be here? It seemed incredible, but still . . . had my best friend shifted her loyalty to Halcyon?

That thought bothered me a lot, but it was nothing compared to the jolt I got the next day. Halcyon's parents called to say they'd received an invitation to visit friends on the West Coast. Since they needed to go out anyway on business, they'd like to accept. But here came the big gut-grabber. Could they drop off Halcyon a little early, on their way?

"Mom!" I wailed when she told me. "You didn't agree, did you?"

"Well, yes. Laurel's going back early to catch up on work, as you know, so the room's free. I can't see any conflict."

"I can! My party! This means Halcyon will be here, butting in and probably making cracks about how Pom Pon went out with saddle shoes. You know how she is!"

Mom absently picked up Laurel's bottle of aspirin and set it down again. "Calm down, Clara. You'll manage. It's up to you to do the best you can to make the party a success. It's all in your hands."

As it turned out, my party's success was in the hands of fate. And those hands were lousy with cold germs.

FIFTEEN

I STARTED FEELING AWFUL THE NIGHT BEFORE THE party. The next morning I wasn't sure I could pull myself together, much less my room where most of the party would take place. It needed rearranging to make room for the girls' sleeping bags.

Feeling feverish and somewhat dizzy, I pushed my bed from the middle of the room over against the wall. The effort made me so weak I wanted to cry. I sat on the floor, my palm against my moist forehead.

Halcyon walked into the room. "What's the matter with you?"

"I don't feel so well."

"I'll go get your mother."

"No!" Mom would take my temperature, and it had to be around a hundred. "I'll be all right. Besides, she's gone to the store for things for the party."

"Oh, that's right, it's tonight, isn't it?"

She knew very well when it was. Halcyon walked over to my dresser, fingered several things and then sprayed on some French cologne Skip had given me for Christmas. "I used to like this brand," she said, "before everyone started using it."

I was so peeved, along with being feverish, that I blurted out, "What are your plans for tonight? Going out?"

"I *was* going over to Angel's, but now I don't know. She's not very dependable, is she?"

"Angel?"

"So I guess I'll just stick around. I think your mother would feel better, having me sort of on deck, since she's going to the city." Halcyon wandered toward the door. "Why does a woman her age want to see the *Nutcracker?* I mean!" She looked upward.

"Mom bought the tickets for us—Laurel and me—but now she's taking a couple of friends." I got up. "And by the way, Halcyon, you needn't bring my mom's age into every conversation. It's kind of crude."

"Well! Excuse *me!*" she said, and then she left.

I almost called her back. I needed Halcyon in a way. But it would have meant overlooking her attitude, and I just couldn't bring myself to do that.

At our early makeshift dinner, I tried my best to be alert and cheery, but the truth was I was feeling worse by the minute. I had to force down the little I ate.

Mom looked at me. "Are you all right?"

"She's just excited, Mrs. Conrad," Halcyon said. "Aren't you, Clara?"

"That's right."

"And I think she's worried about the weather," Halcyon said. "It's snowing, and you have that long drive into Chicago."

124

For once, I was grateful for Halcyon's take-over conversation.

"I have snow tires," Mom said, "and anyway, I'll be home before it gets really bad outside. Ah, Chicago weather."

"New York's as bad," Halcyon said.

I couldn't believe she'd actually said that.

By ten o'clock the party was in full swing, and so was my fever. Halcyon, who could really be helpful when she felt like it, got things together in the kitchen. I took up the supplies of soft drinks and bowls of chips and pretzels. I could hardly make my way across the room because of the bodies draped everywhere. Most girls had already changed into their so-called sleeping gear. Beth Meyers had on a tan fuzzy cover-all that made her look like a teddy bear, and Leanne wore a slinky number that brought whistles until she covered up with a robe. Most of the crew, though, lounged around in oversized T-shirts and underpants. I was still in my jeans and top.

On about my fifth trip upstairs, I couldn't even get into the room because a few of the extroverts were doing a replay of a really dumb skit from speech class, and there was a lot of milling around. I sprawled in the doorway, leaning against the side. The room seemed to be shifting a little. I closed my eyes. The sounds in the room changed and drifts of conversation came to me, mostly of the and-then-he-said-to-me variety. I edged slightly into the room. My stomach sent up a warning signal.

I heard someone thump-thumping up the stairs and I knew it could only be Halcyon. And so it was.

"Dearheart, come on in," I said, waving a limp hand.

She stood eyeing me. "Clara, have you been *drinking?*" I loved that shock in her voice. I'd never heard it before. "You know, your mother . . ."

"Sure, I know my mother." Something told me to crawl out into the hall. Halcyon knelt beside me, probably to smell my breath.

"I'm sick," I moaned. "I think . . ." My stomach gave a lurch.

She grabbed my shoulders and half pulled me into the bathroom. Nothing happened.

Halcyon felt my head. "You're burning up," she said. "You really have got a fever."

I could hear the phone ringing. "Get that, would you? If it's Mom, don't tell her."

"Okay. Just stay there, okay? I'll be right back."

I heard Halcyon thumping down the stairs. The room stopped spinning, and the noise from my room sort of subsided, and then I heard someone say, "Where's Clara?"

"Probably getting more cokes. It's about all she's done all evening. What a bore! I can see why Angel didn't show up."

"I don't think that's it." The voice sounded clear, yet far away. "Why should Angel stay friends with Clara after the way she ripped off her boyfriend?"

"Clara didn't take Skip away from Angel," someone else said.

I didn't, I thought. It just happened.

"That's right," someone said for me. "Don't blame Clara. It could've happened to any girl elected captain. Well, any girl within *reason*."

"I don't believe it could've happened to just anyone," another voice spoke up. "We all know Skip set it up. He passed the word to one of the guys, and he passed it on to someone in Pom Pon that Clara was it. His choice. And so that's why it happened."

You knew, my brain was frantically insisting. You knew all along.

"Sure, Clara's cute, and she was Skip's first choice." It was Mindy's voice. "He told Gary and Gary made me promise to do what I could. But we all know if Clara had lost, Skip would have switched to the winner."

A lot of garbled voices then, with one coming through. "Yeh, probably Liz. But don't tell Clara. That would be mean."

My brain had finally sorted out a message and what it was saying was *Now. Now's the time to be sick.*

I was.

It seemed that everything I'd swallowed, including my pride, was on recall. Afterwards, I felt so weak I could hardly lean over the sink to rinse my face and mouth.

Halcyon came back. "You okay?"

I reached for a towel. "Yeh. Was that my mother?"

"No. It was one of the boys. They're having a party down the street and they might come over."

"No way! Did you say so?"

"Who am I to issue orders? I sent Erica down to try to talk them out of it."

"Tell her to do more than try." The last person in the world I wanted to see right now was Skip. "What time is it?"

"Nearly one."

"One! My mom should be home by now."

"She has to drive those other women home, remember? And it's snowing and blowing outside. You'd better go lie down."

"Okay."

"What if the guys do come over?" There was a worried note in her voice.

"Halcyon, take over! Go get on the phone and tell them not to!" I staggered off to Mom's room.

Lying there, drifting in and out of feverish sleep, I was aware of the girls going up and down the stairs and a lot of squeals and commotion. But through it all what I'd overheard earlier kept going over and over in my thoughts. It was a bad dream come true.

Someone was undressing me. I flung out my arms and fought until I realized it was Mom, and then I asked, "What time is it?"

"Nearly three. The car wouldn't start after the ballet, and I had trouble finding an all-night garage."

"Did you get home okay?" I asked, sitting up. I felt dizzy and disoriented. "Oh. I guess you did. But I was worried."

"I tried to call, but the phone was busy for two solid hours. I'm really annoyed with your friends. Here, let me pull off those jeans."

"You didn't yell at them, did you?" Actually, I didn't care. It was really quiet now. "You didn't send them home, did you?"

"No. I took pity on their parents. But in the morning, out they go. Such carryings on!"

I slept the night with Mom, and the next day, after she'd cleared out the girls and cleaned up the room, she moved me back to my own bed. "I didn't realize that twelve girls could make such a mess," she said. "I even found a peanut butter and jelly sandwich crammed under the cushion of your chair."

"Did they have a good time?" I asked, sinking against the cool pillow.

"You throw a swell party," she said dryly. "Even in absentia." She put a thermometer into my mouth. "I described your symptoms to the doctor, and he said it sounds like flu and to do the usual routine. I'm going out for some things and I want you to stay put. Halcyon can take over while I'm gone."

For once, no for twice, Halcyon's take-over qualities were of some use. She hadn't, at least, let the boys come over last night.

I was awfully sick for a couple of days. Mom managed to talk the doctor into stopping by, but all he said was that I should get plenty of rest, drink fluids, and keep on taking the medicine.

It was okay at first, because I was mostly out of it anyway, but when I started feeling better I got restless. I wanted to hear Skip's voice and try to believe that what I'd overheard was all a mistake, that he really liked me for myself. But in a way, I was afraid. I *knew*.

"Mom," I complained one time, as she came in with my juice, "I keep hearing the phone ring, but I don't know what's going on. Can't I go downstairs?"

"The girls just call to see how you are," she said.

Girls. I drank the juice and wiped my mouth. "Have . . . uh . . . any boys called?"

"He's called once or twice that I know of." Mom gave the slightest flicker of a smile. "Didn't Halcyon tell you?"

"No. So that's why I'd like to get up and answer the phone myself."

"In a day or two. In the meantime, I'll ask Halcyon to jot down all messages."

That hit me wrong. Sure, Halcyon had been nice the night of the party, but that didn't mean I trusted her with my personal calls. "Mom, if you appoint her to phone duty, by the time I'm better I won't have any friends left!"

"Now, Clara, that's just silly. Halcyon can't take away your friends. You should know that."

Yeh, Mom, I thought. You don't know her technique. I visualized the ring. That expensive looking ring with the tiny blue stone. "Has Angel called?"

"Every day. I talked to her myself, a little while ago. Since you're no longer contagious, I told her it would be all right if she stopped by this afternoon. If you feel up to it."

"I do!"

Mom took the empty glass and left the room.

I told Angel about the party—what I remembered of it. Next, I wanted to work the conversation around to Skip and ask Angel's opinion of what I'd overheard, but I wasn't sure how to get started. I decided to warm her up first on her favorite topic, rats.

"Two more weeks and then the big event, eh?" I said, sitting cross-legged up in bed. "Think you'll win first prize at the Fair?"

Carefully, Angel selected a chocolate from a big two-pound box Laurel had sent when she heard I was sick. "Fergy and I aren't concerned about winning," she said. "Although we wouldn't blushingly refuse the prize, if offered. The point is, we've proved it can be done."

"What can?"

"Animal behavior can be shaped, Clara. Goodness. What do you think Fergy and I have been doing all this time?"

"Do you like him?"

Angel looked at me strangely, as though the fever had fried my brains. "What do you mean, like him?"

"As a boy."

She put down the candy box. "Fergy's not a *boy*. I'm not even sure he's a *human*. He's a brain, Clara, a brain. A brain that attached itself to a body so it could move from place to place."

"So you don't like him?"

"I like him, I like him. But I don't *like* him."

I knew what she meant. Now we were warmed up. "Did you like Skip?"

"Skip?" Angel frowned slightly, as though the name had surfaced from a faraway past.

"That's not really what I want to know." I picked out the empty tissue cups from the box and crumpled them. "Do you think he likes me just because I'm Pom Pon captain?"

"Why, of course."

I'd known, even before the evening of the party I'd known, but the shock still must have shown.

For once Angel looked rattled. "I thought you realized . . ."

"Realized what?"

She shrugged. "The way he is."

"What's that supposed to mean?"

"It means . . . Skip chooses winners."

Winners. Was I a winner? I didn't feel like one at the moment. "So," I finally said, "it's true. If Liz had been chosen, Skip would have . . ."

131

"He saw to it that *you* were." Angel was trying to be a comfort. "He liked you best, and he arranged it."

After a few swallows, I said, "I guess I should feel honored."

Angel didn't say anything.

"I mean, he did choose me."

"That's right."

"But the girls didn't. Not really. It was a fake. The whole thing was a fake."

Angel was quiet for a moment. "Don't feel bad. The girls have minds of their own. And you did get the vote."

"But I'm not sure of anything any more. I'm not sure that I have any friends. Real friends." I looked at her. "Even one."

"Clara!" Angel looked shocked. "Could you ever doubt . . . ! I mean, we've both been busy, but no matter what, we're still best, true friends."

I knew she meant it. I hated myself for ever doubting.

She leaned forward and touched my hand. I looked at her fingers. "Where's the ring?"

Angel put her hand to her face and laughed. "Halcyon asked for it back. She said her mother had a fit because actually it's a family heirloom. Can you believe it?"

I could. But I didn't understand. "If that's true, why would she give you the ring in the first place?"

"To make a show. Poor Halcyon. She wants so much to be noticed and admired."

"Huh. For sure."

"It would be so much better if she'd just relax," Angel said. "Underneath Halcyon's not all that bad."

"Mmmm." True, maybe, but I wasn't feeling too sympathetic. "So she took it back, just like that?"

Angel nodded. "Halcyon said she'd give me something else instead."

"Well," I said, "you've always looked good in knee socks."

SIXTEEN

THE QUESTION THAT NOW LOOMED IN MY FEEBLE, fevered little brain was, should I call Skip? But if so, what would I say? *Is it true you set me up as Captain?* I knew it to be true, so the only question was *why.* Dummy, I knew that too. He thought I was the cutest girl on Pom Pon. So let it go. What did it matter? No one knew that I knew except Angel, and she'd never tell. Once I shook off this cold and got the sap running in my system, I'd go out there at half time and prove to everyone that I was a winner—not by election, but naturally.

That settled, I was up the next day and feeling steadier than I'd expected.

"Want to come to the cellar?" Angel asked. "Fergy and I could use your help. We're doing the final run-throughs on the rats. We'll pick the best and put them into heavy training. It's showdown time at the old corral."

I wasn't sure I felt *that* steady. "How about Halcyon helping?"

"She made up with one of the girls and went over to her house. You don't have to handle the rats—Jay Frank likes to do that. Just jot down the times for us on the record sheet."

The cellar was all bright lights and business. Jay Frank was hopping around poking his finger into cages, and Fergy was testing the food-pellet-dropping thing.

"Hello, Sicko," he greeted me. "What brings you to our little laboratory?" (He pronounced it la-*bore*-a-tory.)

"Angel. To help. But I'm not a rat-handler, remember that."

"Don't worry about it," Fergy said. "As a rule, animals don't contract human diseases." He took off his glasses and rubbed them with the bottom of his T-shirt. It looked like an old paint rag. "We started to mix up more dye for the rats—they're fading—but we didn't have all the colors. So, later. Hey, Jay, you ready?"

"I get to bring the rats over to the run, one at a time," Jay Frank told me. "That's my job. They couldn't do it without my help."

I turned to Fergy. "He can't do it during the fair. Who are you going to sucker into doing it then?"

"The job's open," Fergy said. "So if you're interested . . ."

I sneezed. "Let's get going here."

They brought out the rats one by one, set each behind the starting barricade, then lifted it and set the stop-watch. In spite of myself, I got interested. It was kind of cute, the way each little rat took off down the runway, paused at the end, and pressed the lever. I marked each one's time on the sheet.

"Shall we give Little Blue another chance?" Angel

asked Fergy, as Jay Frank handed her the rat with a tinge of blue dye on its head.

"He deserves another chance," Jay Frank pleaded. "He's such a friendly little fellow."

"Amiability cuts no ice in the field of science," Fergy said. "It's the track record that counts."

"Give him a try," Jay Frank still pleaded.

"Yeh, Fergy," I said, "keep an open mind."

"All right, but remember, we're picking the consistently best five performers today for intensive training, and your little pet there is way down on the list, Jay Frank. Put him in position."

Jay Frank did. Fergy raised the barricade and Angel clicked the stop-watch. It ticked on and on as Little Blue sat happily cleaning his whiskers.

"He's hopeless, and never mind prodding with the finger, there, J.F.," Fergy said. "Take him out and, Clara, cross off his name."

"You can't do that to Little Blue!" Jay Frank cried out.

"We're not doing anything to him," Fergy explained. "Just letting him be his own rat-person, as it were. Look at it this way, Jay Frank. Little Blue is not cut out for show biz, but that doesn't make him any less a rat."

"He'll be happier, leading a quiet life, out of the limelight," Angel added.

Jay Frank held Little Blue up to his cheek. "But I love him."

"Then take him," Fergy said. "Compliments of the house."

"Really? For my very own? Oh, Little Blue!" After another round of nuzzling, Jay Frank said, "I need a cage."

Angel sighed. "Take a cage. That small one."

From the look she gave Fergy, I could tell that even her super patience was wearing thin.

It wore even thinner as time went on because Jay Frank, engrossed with Little Blue, had to be reminded each time to bring out a new rat for tryouts and then to return it to its cage.

"It's just as well the fair is two weeks away," Angel said.

"There's a lot of work ahead of us," Fergy said, "making the signs and setting up the display and then transporting all these animals and equipment out of here."

"I'm going home now," Jay Frank said.

I went upstairs with him and, when I saw it was turning dark, was about to offer to walk him home. Instead I sneezed. "Tell you what," I said. "You start out, Jay Frank, and I'll dial your number, and then I'll count to see how long it takes you to answer."

He still liked games, anyone could see, by the quick interest in his eyes. "Okay."

"Button your coat. Go!"

I saw him whisk by the window, and then I dialed. The phone rang and rang. Had he dropped the key in the snow? Was there . . . something . . . someone . . . ? Finally, he answered.

"What took you so long?"

"I couldn't answer because Little Blue jumped right out of my pocket and ran into a stack of dirty clothes on the floor. He's fast, Clara, when he wants to be!"

"Stupid! Why didn't you carry him in the cage?"

"Because it's cold outside!"

Almost on cue, I sneezed again.

"See," Jay Frank said in triumph. "I don't want him to be like you. Sick."

"Turkey!" I hung up and went back to bed.

By the time school started again, I was feeling better. More or less. There were still times when I'd feel warm and other times cool. I felt the same way about Skip. Cool when I thought of how he'd set me up without saying so, and yet warm when he paid attention to me. There was no denying Skip was cute. But that's what he'd said I was. I was beginning to think of cute as a four-letter word.

With the semester coming to a close in three weeks, though, and all the fun things like reviews and tests, I had more than cuteness on my mind. Also, the science fair was scheduled for the same time as the big regional games, which was not a masterpiece of planning on the part of the school.

And as though the tests, science fair, and games weren't enough on their own, Liz suddenly came up with what she called a dynamite variation to one of our Pom Pon routines.

"It's a step I learned at my disco dance class," she said. "Watch . . . let me show you how we could work it right into this number and give it more glitz." She paused. "Miss Curry said it's okay with her if it's okay with all of you."

"We don't have enough time to go messing around. We've got the number down pat, and it's good enough," Erica said.

Liz, who had looked dewy with excitement, faded as more and more comments blasted out.

"Oh, hey, you guys," I heard myself saying. "We're not so hot that we couldn't stand some improvement. Let's see what she has in mind, okay?"

138

Liz shot me a glance of gratitude. I had to give her a lot of credit. In front of those negative faces, she got up and did some really tricky steps that made the routine come alive.

"Great!" I shouted, as she held the last position, although inside, my thoughts were dit-dash-ditting the message, *Clara, you're putting yourself on the line.*

"Yeh," voices around me were echoing. "That looks glitzy all right. But can we learn it?"

Liz, face flushed, said, "The captain has the variations, so she'll need some practice. The squad just does the basic stuff." My heart sank. "I'll show you, Clara, and work with you until you get it down pat, and I'll be with the squad and work with them, too. We can wrap it up in a few sessions."

The squad came along just fine, but I had to work and work. I wasn't a natural the way Liz was.

"Watch," she'd say to me, all patience. "I'll do it in slow motion."

I'd watch and copy. Then we'd speed it up a little and then a little more, until finally I was a repeat pattern of Liz. Still, she was the natural.

"Would you want to lead this one routine?" I asked her. "I wouldn't mind. Honestly."

"You're fine," she said. "Trust yourself." She wasn't such a bad kid.

One night at practice we did the new number when the team and a few scattered parents, come to drive their kids home, were sitting around on the bleachers. As we were trotting off to the locker room afterwards, someone standing behind a pillar grabbed me off to the side.

"Skip, hi!" I hated to think how I looked. Perspiration was actually stinging my eyes.

"A real class act you got there," he said. "You looked real cute."

That word did it. "I'm not cute," I said.

"No?" The slow smile built up and his eyes . . what can I say except that they seemed to caress me more than ever?

"I look lousy, I feel lousy," I said. "But I *am* captain. That's what counts, isn't it?"

"Whatever." Skip's look had shifted to the coach out on the floor, who was whistling to the team. "See you later."

"Skip," I reached out to grab his sleeve, but since his arm was bare, the grab turned into a pinch. "What if I'd lost the election? That you set up?"

He rubbed the spot on his arm, which was turning a spidery pink. "You're cuckoo. I've gotta go. Coach is . . ."

I reached out to really pinch him this time, only he ducked. "You're cute, Clara, as I said. But don't press your luck." He gave me an almost hostile look, then trotted out to the team.

I stood there thinking, What's your problem, Clara? What are you doing? *Don't press your luck,* he'd said. *You can be replaced,* he hadn't said, though wasn't it true? And so smart, cute Clara had verbally and physically attacked the guy who was only the prize catch of Harrison Junior High. Why? I asked myself. Is it some kind of crime that he likes you and what you stand for?

But what is it that I stand for, I thought, as I went back to the lockers. What am I, exactly?

I'm the captain. I'm Skip's girl. The words whirled around in my mind. I wondered if the fever was coming back. There must be something wrong with me, else why would I have lashed out at Skip like that? He'd liked me enough to get me elected captain so he could go out with me. I should be flattered. I should be grateful. Instead, I had a terrible feeling of wanting to punch someone. Mostly myself.

We kept the disco steps in the routine and continued practicing for the first regional game, coming up the next week on Wednesday. Once in a while, leading the variations, I'd get a glimpse of Liz, doing the simpler steps with the rest of the squad, but then I'd look away. Fair is fair, as they say. But not always.

Skip continued to call every night, as though that little scene by the bleachers had never taken place. "I like that dance thing you're doing," he said one evening. "Who came up with that idea?"

I hesitated. *It just developed,* I wanted to say. "Liz," I said. "Liz thought of it."

Now there was silence from Skip's end. "It's great," he said then. "I like it. You look like a real knockout, Clara."

Something inside of me murmured, is that it? Is that where it's at? But all I said was, "Thank you."

Meanwhile, back in the cellar, things were moving right along. Fergy and Angel dismantled the run and took it over to the school, along with all the materials for the display set-up.

The rats, meanwhile, were still confined to quarters in our cellar. "We've got to shield them until show time," Fergy explained. "Because all that attention from the crowds might affect their performance."

"Yeh, like they keep rock stars locked in hotel rooms with security guards," I said. "But that's to protect them from the groupies, which doesn't apply in this case."

"Anyway, it's nice of you to offer to feed them tonight while Angel and I are over setting up the display."

"I'm feeding them?"

"Thanks, I accept the offer," Fergy said quickly. "Just what I lay out, though, don't give them any more. We'll pick them up at six tomorrow for the grand opening at seven." He said this with a look at his watch and mine, as though we had to synchronize.

During a free hour the next afternoon, I got a pass to go to the chemistry lab, where the kids were setting up the science fair stuff, on the pretext that I had some vital information for Angel. Actually, I just wanted to wish her luck and to hear her reassure me that I wouldn't louse up the routine during the game. My knees were already shaking, just from my thinking of the crowds that would be there. I mean, this was a killer game.

Angel wasn't around, but there was Halcyon, fastening up rat photos. "How come you're doing that?" I asked.

"Because they go along with the experiment."

It was like my own words on the plane coming back. I'd just meant them as comfort to Halcyon at the time, but boy, she'd jumped on them. When the experiment took first prize, she'd take a lot of credit. Oh, well. "Are you going with Angel and Fergy to pick up the rats?" I asked her. "Or will you give them your key to get in?"

"I'll probably be tied up here. I left the house unlocked. Hold up these two photos so I can step back and see which way they should face."

Face them against the wall was what I wanted to say, but I held them up.

"Higher," Halcyon commanded. "Can't you stop jiggling?"

"I'm jumpy. Our game starts at five. C'mon, Halcyon, decide."

"Oh, all right, go." Halcyon heaved a sigh. "Listen, this game happens to be . . ."

"Clara, we've heard that so many times. Here, give me those photos."

I tossed them onto the table and left.

After school, the Pom Pon squad gathered in the locker room and we got into our outfits. Then we went through the routines, with special emphasis on the disco variation. After about the third time, Miss Curry told us to knock it off, we'd peak before our performance.

While the girls were relaxing, she called me aside. "Clara, I guess this is as good a time to tell you as any. I was dubious last fall about putting you on the squad at all, considering your lack of experience. But I decided to play a long shot. Then, when you were elected captain, I confess I had serious doubts." She combed her fingers through her short hair. "It was unusual, to say the least . . . a newcomer. But again, I thought you'd either come through or drop out altogether."

I waited, wondering what she was leading up to.

"Well, you've come through. You've got a spark. The girls have a real live leader, and the crowd out there today is in for a treat." She squeezed her eyes at me. "Give them a good show."

I stood, tugging at my sweater cuffs, not knowing what to say. Someone came to the door and called, "Ten minutes."

Everyone started squealing, checking outfits, knotting shoe laces, looking in mirrors, or making

143

mad dashes to the john. My heart was thump-thump-thumping, and I could feel a trickle of perspiration toward my bra.

"Okay, girls, this is it," Miss Curry said, checking her watch. "We'll go out and stand in the areaway to be ready. The band plays the national anthem, the principal will say a few words over the mike, then we go on. Let's hit it, girls! Mindy, put that comb away. All out!"

We filed out of the locker room and down a corridor and then into a side door of the gym. Walls of bleachers were on each side. People near the end looked us over.

The band started playing the national anthem. Everyone stood up. We, of course, were already standing, but I want to tell you I thought my legs were going to fold like a card table's any minute.

"Sing," I told myself. "Lose yourself in the anthem." But it was hard to jump in because the people on one side of us were a couple of words behind the ones on the other side, and they were all lagging behind the band.

". . . bursting in air . . . gave proof . . ." I chimed in, just to keep my teeth from chattering.

The girl next to me gave me a jab, and I stopped. I didn't think I'd sounded that bad.

"Clara . . ." she whispered. She pointed back of us, a worried look on her face. I turned. Some boy, with a piece of paper in his hand, was coming forward as the girls stared.

"Clara Conrad?" the boy asked.

Oh, say does th—at star spangled . . . they sang.

"What?" I felt chilled as I stared at the boy.

"There's a phone call for you in the main office."

"I can't leave!" *. . . still wa—ve . . . o'er the land*

144

. . . "We've got to go out there in a couple of minutes! Who is it? What is the call?"

The kid hunched his shoulders. "How should I know? They just said to come get you, it's urgent. Yeh, urgent."

Miss Curry had come up and heard the last. She took the paper, put her hand on my shoulder, and said, "Hurry, honey. Go see what it's about. There's time, the principal's long-winded." She was leading me out to the corridor as she talked. "If it's an emergency, do what you need to do. We'll cover all right." She squeezed my shoulder. "But hurry." She rushed back to the girls, and I raced up the steps and down the hall toward the office. Mom . . . I thought. Something's happened to Mom. Or to Laurel. Something awful.

I dashed into the office, and the secretary silently held up the phone. It slipped in my grip, and I steadied my wrist with the other hand. "Hello?"

Nothing.

"Hello? *Hello!*"

And then the voice came through, scared and little. It was Jay Frank. "Help," he said. "Clara, help." And that was all.

SEVENTEEN

W HAT IS IT?" I GASPED INTO THE PHONE. "TELL me!"

Silence. Just awful silence.

I took the phone from my ear and stared at it dumbly. And then I looked at the anxious face of the secretary. "I've got to leave," I said through the shaking that had started up in my chest. I slammed down the receiver. "Something . . . terrible . . ." I started for the door. "Tell them," I yelled over my shoulder, "tell them . . . anyone who asks . . ."

"Sweetheart, you can't run out like that. Take this." A coat was flung over my shoulders. "Could I drive you?"

But I was already racing down the hall and out of the building. With the coat flapping at my heels as I clutched it around me, I started running the several blocks home. Jay Frank alone in the house, always scared about monsters and stupid things, but never, never would he call me unless there was a very real kind of danger! A little boy alone, in the gathering

dark, and on this day with no one around, someone
. . . knowing . . . waiting?

I rounded the corner and ran straight for Jay
Frank's house. Sweating, scared half to death, and
with no idea of what I'd do once inside, I grabbed at
the back door handle. Locked. I shook the door.
Locked tight.

I tore around to the front of the house and rattled
and jangled that door. Locked like a fort. I rang the
bell and yelled, "It's me, Jay Frank! Let me in!"

I tried to look through an opening in the front
curtains, but it was dark inside. Why hadn't Jay
Frank turned on the light, first thing, like always?
Because there was someone in there with him. The
thought made me pull back and moan with fear. Oh,
Jay Frank!

The police! I'd have to go home and call the
police. Oh, let me be in time! Gasping for air
through my mouth, I cut over toward our back door.
About halfway there, I remembered my purse and
my key were back at school! But I ran for the door
anyway. I'd break it down, or break a window,
or . . .

The door was open.

I rushed into the kitchen, dropped the coat, and
picked up the phone.

"Oh," a voice said behind me. "You finally got
here."

The phone dropped from my hand and dangled
on its coiled cord as I whirled around. "Jay Frank!
Jay Frank!" I thought I'd collapse. "Are you all
right?" I dropped to my knees and clutched his
shoulders.

"Well," he said, "I'm pretty worried."

I felt kind of dazed. *Worried* didn't seem quite the

147

word. "What's happened? Was someone after you?
Tell me!" I glanced toward the open door.

"You're so funny, Clara. Who would be after
me?"

"You called! You called *HELP!* What's wrong?" I
gave him a little shake.

"It's a long story. Why don't we sit down?"

I stared at him, dazed. He was all right. And I'd
left everything . . . my *life* . . . and come running.

"It's very confusing," Jay Frank sighed. "Say,
why are you wearing that outfit?"

I bent my head and covered my face with my
hands. They'd be out on the floor by now. The Pom
Pon girls in their short pleated skirts and their
sweaters, doing their opening routine. Liz would be
leading them, and the crowd would be hyped up and
the girls would be even more so. And they'd flash
and dip and dance and bedazzle . . .

Jay Frank made a little throat-clearing sound. "Do
you want to go back, and I'll tell you about it later?"

I lifted my head. I felt numb. "You might as well
give me the story, now that I'm here." I couldn't go
back. It was too late. They had gone on without me,
and I'd never live it down. "What's happened, Jay
Frank?"

"Well." He sat sideways on a kitchen chair and
hooked one heel on the rung. "You know Little
Blue."

*Don't hit him. He's only a child. A child you prac-
tically raised, so who's to blame.* "Tell me," I said,
falling onto the opposite chair and leaning forward
on my arms on the table. "Tell me about Little
Blue."

Jay Frank licked his thin lips and gave me the
kind of look he always gives when he's testing the

148

air, so to speak. "Well," he said, still feeling his way, "he hasn't seemed happy these last few days."

Was I really sitting here in the kitchen, decked out in my Pom Pon outfit, listening to this? *Little Blue is not in a happy frame of mind.* I stared for several seconds, and then in an oh-so-steady voice inquired, "And what seems to be troubling Little Blue?"

Jay Frank's look was still wary. "I had to show him, Clara. I had to show him he could do it if he really tried. But you see, I ran into a problem."

He'd warned me it was a long story. My life was shot. I had all the time in the world now. "You want to take it step by step, Jay Frank? Tell me all about Little Blue and his search for happiness. Don't spare the slightest detail."

He told me. Little Blue, it seems, had been languishing alone in his cage, his little rat-heart despondent, ever since he had been phased out of the semifinals. So in a last-ditch effort to shore up the creature's spirits, Jay Frank had brought him over to our house to do the run again, to prove he still had the stuff. But, lo, the run had been removed. So Jay Frank had had to improvise another, out of bricks and pieces of wood.

"Stop!" I said. "Don't tell me. Your rat jumped the run and now he's loose in our basement!" I shoved back my chair with a sigh. "All right, let's go look." I felt a million years old.

"No! That's not it at all. He's in the cage where I put him."

I was finally getting irritated. No, not irritated. More like rabid. "So! Get to the point! What's the big emergency, huh? You call me at the office, yell

Help! and get me crazy, and now you tell me what? That your dumb rat's in a cage, where he belongs!"

"Clara, there's a problem. I'm trying to tell you. I put him in a cage with another rat. And now . . . and now . . ."

"And now *what?*"

". . . I can't tell which is which!"

If ever there was a dead silence, this was it.

"You see," Jay Frank said, pulling in on his lips, "they'll be coming to get the five champions pretty soon. And you know how they said they were going to put fresh dye on their heads? Well they haven't, yet . . . and now . . ."

Good-bye Pom Pon, Good-bye Year of the Clara. Good-bye happiness. All done in by an undyed rat.

"Clara . . ." From somewhere beyond my closed eyes Jay Frank's voice coaxed. "Can you help me? Angel and Fergy will be so mad. And they are my friends."

I opened my eyes. "Your friends! And yet, you called *me.*"

He looked at me solemnly. "But you are my first, best friend."

The anger and frustration drained right out of me. He was only a kid, a pesty little kid, but he had a hold on my life. I stood up and held out my hand. I had all the time in the world, now. "Come on, then. Let's go down and see if we can sort them out. You really can't tell which is which, huh?"

"I think I can." He let go of my hand to start down the steps. "But then I think I'm wrong. If I'd only just put him in Little Yellow's cage instead of Little Violet's!"

If only.

If only the phone call had come five minutes later,

I would have been unreachable. I would now be radiant, hyped up, wowing the crowds. But here I was instead. In the cellar.

Jay Frank reached into the first cage, took out the mixed up pair, and held one rat in each hand under a bright light. The dye was indistinct. I got a magnifying glass from upstairs and moved it back and forth over each squirmy head. "I'm pretty sure this one's blue," I said finally. "See those hairs there . . . no right here . . ."

"Yes, you're right! Oh, my Little Blue, I love you so." Jay Frank snuggled it to his face. "How could I ever have mixed you up with that regular rat?"

"Will you please shove Mister Regular back into his cage?" I asked. "Hey, when I said shove, I didn't mean literally," I said, as the rat rolled over. "And Jay Frank," I said, latching the cage, "there's an old saying, 'It's a wise mother who knows her own child.' In your case you'd better play it safe with an old felt marker."

"Little Blue doesn't need a mark any more," Jay Frank said. "I know who he is. And he does, too. He'll be all right now."

"Good-bye, then," I said.

"Bye, Clara." He started for the stairs. "Thank you."

Thank you. That was it. *Thank you.* My world shot, and he says *thank you.*

I stared at the five rat cages in a row. They could have been anything. They were nothing to me. Just five rat cages in a row. I stood there for I don't know how long, nothing special in my mind. I felt like nothing.

Suddenly I heard a car door slam, and voices—

Angel, Fergy, and whoever was driving. If they saw
me here, in my Pom Pon outfit, there'd have to be
all kinds of questions, explanations, and then all
kinds of assurances that it wasn't Angel's and Fergy's
fault. I wasn't up to it at the moment. Like a flash,
I tore upstairs, across the kitchen, and halfway up
the other stairs before pausing.

". . . thank goodness Halcyon remembered to
leave the door open," I heard Angel say. Then the
voices drifted downward.

They were in the cellar for quite a while, probably
cleaning the cages and putting fresh dye on the
champion rat heads. Little did they dream what the
dye delay had done to me, or how close they'd come
to carting off a loser because of a happiness crisis.

After the final door slam and the sound of the car
leaving, I sank to the steps. It didn't matter that my
pleated Pom Pon skirt was too short for that kind
of sitting. I was alone in the house. Man, was I ever
alone. Like Little Blue, I'd missed out on the main
event.

They'd be well into the game by now. I could
almost see the team pounding down the court, sinking basket after basket as the crowd went berserk.
And the Pom Pon squad, exploding out to the floor
in a burst of color and dazzle, whipping the crowd
into even further frenzy with its routines.

I shifted, putting my back against the wall and
propping a sneakered foot against the banister. I
knew I should go back, but what for? They didn't
need me. Liz could take over just as well. She already had.

In the dusk, I visualized the court again. Skip
. . . dribbling his way down the court, arching his
body and sinking another one into the basket. And

Liz looking at him. And Skip knowing she was look-ing. And liking it?

I must not be myself, sitting here on the stairs, not moving, not really caring. The thought of Skip and Liz together interested me. Yes, interested. Like half-watching a TV show while doing math. Everything seemed so distant and far away. I could almost close my eyes here and doze. Except that I'd proba-bly fall down the stairs.

You've got to go back, I told myself. I didn't want to go back. You've got to go back. I didn't want to go back. Clara! Stop putting things off! I'm telling you to get off your duff and go back. I got up, went to the bathroom, fixed up my face and hair, wrapped myself up in the coat, and trudged back to the school.

"Nothing serious?" the secretary in the office asked, as I thanked her for the use of the coat.

"No. Just a family thing. It's okay now. Who's winning the game?"

"Oh, Clara, I don't know. There's so much com-motion around this place . . ."

I could hear the crowd yelling as I got near the gym. The game must be really going strong. And then there was a mighty roar, and I heard a whistle, and a voice announce, "Half-time!" Now's when they'd do the disco thing.

I could rush out right now and with a grand flourish take over. One part of me wanted to. But it was as though there was a hand on my shoulder and a voice saying, "Let Liz do it. It's her act." And I was so tired.

Standing barely inside the areaway, in the shad-ows, I watched as Liz sprinted out front. The music started, and the squad went through the routine

without missing a beat. After the crowd cheered
some people started off the bleachers for the rest-
rooms or refreshments, and I took off for the locker
room.

In a little while the girls came rushing in, so
caught up in the excitement and afterglow that it
took a couple of minutes for some of them even to
notice me.

"Clara! You missed us! And we were so great!"
Liz rushed over and flung her arms around me.

"I saw you! It really was great."

Liz whirled, face flushed, her body still so keyed
up she couldn't stop the motion.

Miss Curry came in. "Girls, in one word . . .
pow!" she said. "Keep up the pace." And then
"Clara, did something happen at home?"

"Just a family thing. It's okay now."

The girls reclustered around Liz, but she came
back to me. "The second half's all yours," she said
She was still breathing in happy little gasps.

"No, Liz," I heard myself saying. "Keep going."
She was all revved up and my motor hadn't even
turned over. "Finish the game. I'd just like to watch
with the others." The standbys, I meant.

Miss Curry hustled them out, then turned to me
"Clara?"

"Would you mind if I dropped out for today?"

A flicker of concern passed over her face before
she nodded and left. She probably thought there'
been some really big trauma at home.

The second half of the game seemed to flash by
with the Harrison team sinking so many baskets
was ridiculous. The crowd screamed, the chee
sounded, and finally with a long shot from Skip ju
before the whistle, it was all over.

Our group of girls poured out into the areaway, and the team came breaking through. I happened to be one of the first ones out, but still with the group. The team came jogging past. The guys didn't touch their girl friends or anything because of the coach, but they called out little things. All of the guys, that is, except Skip. His eyes swept past everyone, including me.

Mindy noticed. "Boy! What's with him!" She glanced at me. "He looked as though he didn't even recognize you."

I didn't know what to say. "Maybe," I said after a moment, "the blue dye on my forehead has faded, too."

Mindy gave a little laugh, the way kids do when they think they should get it but really don't.

To tell the truth, I really didn't get it myself.

Angel did.

I looked her up, manning the booth alone during the dinner lull at the science fair. We sat on matching high stools next to the cages, and I told her about what had happened at home and at the game. And then I mentioned my remark about the blue dye.

"Oh, Clara!" Angel clasped her hands. "You don't really believe you need some special sign or mark to prove you're somebody, do you?"

"I seem to be nobody now."

"You think Little Blue was a nothing rat just because his color faded? A rat like any other rat?"

I shrugged. Who cared, really?

"Listen, I'd have known in a minute if he'd been brought over by mistake. And you know why?"

"Why?"

"Because Little Blue has a mind of his own," Angel said. "I admire that little thing. He decided

155

one day that he wasn't going to race pell-mell down
the runway just because of the pellet. It wasn't the
most important thing in his life, not at that moment."

"Look, Angel, I'm sorry I ever brought up the
idea of the blue dye. It was just a remark." I shifted
on the stool. "Anyway, as much as you admire Little
Blue's independence and all, it has nothing to do
with me. You see, I do want the prize. I want to be
popular and lead the cheers and be out front more
than anything else in the world."

Angel looked at me and slowly smiled. Then in a
gentle tone she murmured, *"Help."*

I caught my breath, then I relaxed and slowly let
it out. "What could I do?" I said in a small voice.
"Jay Frank needed me. I'm his first, best friend."
Tears misted my eyes. I looked away.

There was silence. Then ever so softly Angel said,
"Clara, you will never need any blue dye. Believe
me."

EIGHTEEN

THAT NIGHT MOM WAS AT ONE OF HER MEET-
ings, Halcyon was hanging around the science fair,
and I was hanging around the house waiting for the
phone to ring. I didn't know what I'd say when he
called. Maybe be cool and let him explain, if he
could. Maybe I'd pretend I had someone there and
couldn't talk and make him crazy.

The phone didn't ring at seven. It didn't ring at
seven-thirty. Or eight.

I started doing a burn. Who did Skip think he
was, anyway, to cut me out in front of all the girls,
and then not even call to try to explain? Now, when
he did get around to calling, I'd have a few choice
things to say, myself.

At eight-thirty Halcyon came home. I was sitting
at the kitchen table, thinking about but not actually
doing my nails.

"How come you're down here?" she asked.

"There's no law against it."

She tossed off her coat, opened the refrigerator,

and took out the milk. "I wouldn't hold my breath, waiting for Skip to call if I were you," she said. She got out a glass and poured the milk.

What could she do . . . look right into my head? "Really." I tried to act unconcerned as I unscrewed the cap of the nail polish.

"He was at the fair. With Liz. Her seventh grade sister has an exhibit."

"Liz!" I looked up and met Halcyon's look. "Liz?"

"Yeh, Liz. She stopped and talked to Angel and Fergy, but Skip just stood off a-ways with that smirk on his face that we all know so well." Halcyon finished the milk and rinsed the glass. "I heard you ducked out of the game. Don't worry, it wasn't on the loudspeaker system or anything like that. Angel told me."

"Oh." I brushed polish on a nail and part of the cuticle, too. Halcyon was hovering somewhere behind me now. I had the feeling she was trying to be decent but couldn't let go enough to face me with it.

"We all . . . Angel and Fergy and I . . . think it was . . ." She cleared her throat. "For Jay Frank . . ." She cleared her throat again. "An okay thing that you did. I mean . . ."

"Thanks." I wanted to turn around, but didn't. I cleaned off the nail with remover. My hand was shaking. "You're sure they were together? Skip and Liz? Not just . . . well . . . ?"

"I'd say they were together. And you know what else I'd say?" She allowed for some silence. "I'd say let Skip find his own level and go out with Liz, if he wants to. You're too good for him anyway."

By the time I'd recovered enough from shock to turn around, Halcyon was gone. For once, she didn't even elephant-thump up the stairs.

It was too much, all at once. Boyfriend turns traitor, enemy turns ally. What could I make of it? Nothing at the moment.

So much for the manicure. I picked up the bottles, gave the phone a dirty look, and went upstairs.

I was lying on my back in bed, arms folded under my head, when I thought of it. The list.

Springing up, I flung open the desk drawer, found the paper, and tore it into little pieces. As they fell in the general direction of the wastebasket, I said, "So much for list-making."

Feeling free, I climbed back into bed, got comfortable, and was just drifting off when Mom came quietly into the room. "Oh, sorry," she said, as I stirred under her light kiss. "I thought you were still . . ."

"That's okay." I took her hand and eased her to the side of my bed. "How was the meeting?"

"All right. I saw Sheri out by the driveway just now with Jay Frank. He's still quite a chatterbox, isn't he?"

"That kid should be in bed. What did he tell you?" I mumbled into the edge of the pillow.

"Bits and scraps. I'd like to hear the story from you in logical sequence. I got the impression that you've been through a lot lately."

"Yeh, in a way."

"Will you tell me about it?"

"Sure, Mom." I yawned.

"Tomorrow night, after your game? No meetings. No paper work. Just you and me."

"And maybe Halcyon," I said. "She's been in on it, too."

I could almost see Mom's eyebrows lift in the

dark, but all she said was, "Whatever." She shifted, touched my hair, and got up.

"Good night, Mom."

"Good night, Clara. Sleep tight."

And together, we said, "Don't let the bedbugs bite."

The next afternoon, I had time before the game to dash into the science fair room again. Angel and Fergy were at the booth together. The judges had been around. There was a red ribbon attached to the display.

"Second place! Oh, no!"

Angel laughed. "Don't look as though we'd been wiped out, Clara."

"But who?" I looked around.

"Tom and Bill did a really great thing on the Voyager I probe of Jupiter," Angel said. "Charts, pictures . . . you should take a look at it."

"But I thought for sure . . ." I went to the cages. "It's not fair. I'll bet those guys had their parents help them."

"Come off it, Clara," Fergy said. "It's not the end of the line. Our show's generated a lot of interest. Some man with college connections even asked us to keep in touch. Right, Angel?"

"Yeh. And Halcyon's floating, too. A *Herald* photographer told her she had the touch."

"Great." I really was glad. "Well, child scientists, I've got to get going. The game . . ."

"Knock 'em out, Captain," Angel said. "Give them the old pizazz."

The word *captain* almost took the starch out of me. "Angel . . ." I motioned her a little away from Fergy. "You once said 'fair is fair.' Remember?"

For possibly the first time in her life, Angel looked uneasy.

"But this whole caper, in a way, wasn't strictly . . . you know?"

"I know." Angel's glance focused somewhere on the floor. "It seemed so reasonable at the time . . . trading what we wanted for what you wanted. But it was a little . . . ummmm . . ."

"Yeh." Everyone had used everyone else. "But, Angel, there's one thing. We did work hard."

"That's right."

"So we shouldn't feel totally bad."

"I don't." Angel gave me a look. "But about Skip . . ."

"Oh, that's something else. I'm going to tell him, but good."

We exchanged girl-type looks. I waved to Fergy and walked out of the room.

And wouldn't you know? Just then I saw Skip coming down the hall. I'm sure he saw me, too, but he turned his head and pretended to brush something off his shoulder as he walked past. He didn't have dandruff. No way. Not with the care he gave his golden locks.

I wasn't going to let him get by. This was my chance. "Hey, Skip!"

He turned and faked a look of surprise.

I hoped my voice wouldn't betray my nervousness. "Nice game you played yesterday," I said, as I caught up with him.

"Oh, thanks." His smile was kind of testing me.

"As it happened, I wasn't around to get the full impact."

Something in my tone faded his smile. "Yeh, I heard. That was a pretty lowdown thing you did, deserting the squad for a nothing reason. And leaving poor Liz . . ."

"Poor Liz did all right."

"Okay, but you're supposed to be captain."

"Yeah. Because you set it up."

His eyes hardened. "I thought you had the stuff."

"Don't give me that *stuff* business. You thought I was *cute*. You thought we'd look cute together!"

"Yeh, well, maybe I've changed my mind."

"No kidding." Boy, my voice dripped with sarcasm.

"Look!" His voice rose with anger. "First you go off during the Thanksgiving dance . . ."

"I! *I* went off! What about . . ."

"And then during Christmas vacation, when we could've got together, you were laying around sick."

"Not *laying. Lying.* I was *lying* around sick."

"And then you pulled that little fadeout yesterday. Kid, I've had it with you."

"You've had it! I've had it!" I shouted. "You can go throw *yourself* through a hoop for all I care." And then as a brilliant after-thought I added, "But you might get stuck in the net, with that big head of yours."

Skip's face turned a deep, furious red. "You can try to cut me down all you want, but just keep in mind that I'm still number one on the team. Think of that when you're sitting on the sidelines."

I wasn't nervous any more. Calmly, steadily, I looked him in the eye and said, "But Skip, I won't be sitting on the sidelines. I'm the Pom Pon captain. Remember? And as captain, I'll be right out front, leading the routines."

He seemed to be struggling for a hotshot comeback, but he fell back on a look of complete con-

162

tempt and a shrug of the shoulders. Then he walked off.

"Don't lose your comb!" I called out.

Instinctively, his hand went back and slapped his hip pocket. Then he really rushed off.

The first half of that day's game didn't go so well for our team. Skip fumbled the ball several times.

As half-time began to loom, I started feeling the old unsureness slip back. What if I led the disco routine and loused it up? Shouldn't I let Liz take over? She was giving me little glances. With a few brief words I could hand it all over. Let someone else do it. Play it safe.

But was this what The Year of the Clara was all about? Wheel and deal, but when it gets really tough, throw in the towel? No, I didn't think so. I'd been on a big popularity binge. Nothing wrong with that. But it had been laid on me. Now was the moment, coming up, to show I'd done at least a little something on my own.

"Clara . . ." Mindy was nudging me. "It's almost half-time. Are you ready?"

"I'm ready, Mindy."

And I was. When the whistle blew, I raced out, pom pons in hand, and the girls raced after me. There was a hush. I smiled, and the team smiled back at me. Every cell in my body was saying, "Let's go!"

The music started, and we went into the routine that had become a part of us. The music quickened, and we swirled, swooped, did the intricate steps all together, all to the beat. And then came the crescendo and the trick finale, and the final beat as we sank to one knee, arms raised toward the crowd, pom pons fluttering. We made it!

We held the pose for the applause.

The cheers felt great, but in a different way this time. I hadn't done it for Skip. I hadn't done it for fame. I'd done it for myself. For me. Clara. And for the school, too. We were in this together.

With the applause still hanging in the air, the girls rushed off, and I followed. It's all over, I thought, as I watched them disappearing into the locker room. The big ring-a-ding-ding is all finished.

But it wasn't! The basketball season was winding up, to be sure, but what did that count in the grand scheme of things? Another semester, and who knew what? There was a big, exciting bunch of stuff whizzing around out there in the world and just anything could happen. Oh, wow, it was all so stupefying!

There in the hall I tossed my pom pons aside and started turning cartwheels. Then I started twirling. "Watch out, world!" I called out, "This time I'm *really* on my way!"

"Clara!"

Hands grasped me. Staggering a little, I saw the wavering figures of Angel and Halcyon.

"What's the matter?" I blinked until they came into focus.

"You're asking *us?*" Halcyon stared. "We came back to say what a smash you were, and here you are, cracking up."

"I'm just . . ."

"Winding down?" Angel asked, helpfully.

"Wrong-o. Winding up."

Halcyon shook her head. "Looney Tunes revisited."

"Oh, well." I picked up the pom pons and slapped

one into each of their hands. "A little souvenir," I said.

"What?"

"Why?"

"The season of the Pom Pon has passed. The *year* is just getting underway."

Neither of them got it, I could tell. But as we walked down the hall together, I didn't go on to explain. Some things you just have to know for yourself. Don't you agree?

ABOUT THE AUTHOR

STELLA PEVSNER began her writing career as a copywriter for a Chicago advertising agency, then moved on as publicity director at a large cosmetics firm. Later she free-lanced until her four children urged her to write children's books. Ms. Pevsner has several award-winning titles which are available from Archway: *And You Give Me a Pain, Elaine,* the winner of a Golden Kite Award; *Call Me Heller, That's My Name,* for which the author won the Chicago Women in Publishing Award; and *Cute Is a Four-Letter Word,* which won a Carl Sandburg Award.

Aside from writing, Stella Pevsner is interested in all kinds of arts and crafts and frequents large art fairs. She also enjoys ballet, and when home from her extensive foreign travels, is active backstage in the community theater.

Ms. Pevsner lives in Palatine, Illinois, with her doctor-husband.